VALIANT REIGN

BROOKE SIVENDRA

Copyright © 2020 by BROOKE SIVENDRA

All rights reserved.

The moral right of Brooke Sivendra to be identified as the author of this work has been asserted by her accordance with the Copyright, Designs and Patents Act 1988.

This is a work of fiction. All the characters in this book are fictitious, and any resemblance to actual persons living or dead is purely coincidental.

No part of this publication may be reproduced, stored in a retrieval system or transmitted in any form or by any means, without the prior permission in writing of the publisher, not to be otherwise circulated in any form of binding or cover other than that in which it is published without a similar condition, including this condition, being imposed on the subsequent purchaser.

Cover by Virtually Possible Designs

Ebook: 978-0-6485688-5-8

Print: 978-0-6485688-4-1

ASHER

"I'm going to execute him," Asher said, turning to stare his brother in the eye. "And then I'm going to destroy Adani. The world is going to see who they really are. I'm going to take everything from them, just like they tried to do to me.

"I'm going to destroy them all," Asher said as a fierce determination rose in his chest. "Adani will fall—and I'm going to take it all."

ASHER'S CHEST heaved as he stared through the glass at the manicured lawns outside the windows. Invisible chains tightened around his chest like being squeezed by a cobra. He'd always known someone was working against him—against Santina—but he'd never expected the threat to come from his cousin.

Troy.

He was the only person Asher had ever heard use that phrase—*velvet stamped*—and it all made sense now.

Troy had accompanied Asher on many official duty trips. He'd been beside Asher when he'd negotiated the last round of aid funding.

Troy is too ambitious.

The memory flooded his mind so clearly that for a moment he thought he'd heard his father whisper it. When King Martin had told Asher he would become Crown Prince, Asher had asked why his father hadn't chosen Troy instead. Troy had military and diplomatic experience and on paper had been a more suitable candidate for the title. His father had responded: *"Troy is too ambitious."*

Had his father had an inkling something wasn't right?

He shook his head, a feeble attempt to shake the question from his mind. He would never know the answer, since his murdered father could never tell him.

Asher sighed heavily as he turned, his eyes landing on his brother, Alistair, who looked like he'd aged ten years in the past few days. His hair was disheveled and his skin grimy from time spent in the cells. His nose was still bruised from Asher punching him, but now Asher felt empathy rather than anger. Alistair was many things . . . but it turned out being a terrible father was not one of them. Asher prayed Alistair's moves had been enough to ensure the boy hadn't been harmed.

"We'll get him back," Asher said, determined. "We will get your son back and he will live here at the palace. I will help you."

Alistair's face crumpled and for the first time in Asher's life, he thought he saw his brother's eyes glisten.

Movement across the room distracted him and he realized Abi was still standing there. She looked between the two brothers uncomfortably.

"I'm going to step out for a moment," she said, and this time Asher let her go.

His eyes followed her, and he noticed Alistair watching him.

"If Martin Snider finds out that I've talked, he'll kill him. Don't think he won't, Asher," Alistair said desperately. "He killed our father. I'm sure of that."

"Then it's a good thing James Thomas is working this case," Asher said, looking to the door. Where *was* James Thomas? Why hadn't he come back to the room?

Asher's stomach churned and he walked to the door. Three guards stood outside, poised and ready to defend their king.

"Where is James?" Asher asked.

"He said he'd be back in a minute," one guard responded, his face giving away nothing.

"How many minutes ago was that?" Asher asked, unsure how long he'd been lost in his thoughts.

"About three, Your Majesty," the guard said.

Asher raised an eyebrow.

Where are you, James Thomas?

Asher didn't like this at all. Surely James could call; why did he need to leave the room?

The office phone rang, echoing through the otherwise silent room, and Asher stepped back inside and answered it.

"King Asher speaking," he said.

"It's James. Put the phone on speaker and give it to Alistair," he demanded.

Asher clicked on the microphone icon and looked to his brother. "It's James," he said slowly.

Alistair glanced dubiously at him and then cleared his throat. "Hello?"

"How did you communicate with Martin Snider?" James asked.

Alistair frowned. "Telephone. I already told you that."

"Which telephone? Because the calls weren't made to your cell phone," James said, matter-of-factly.

Alistair paused for the briefest moment, but Asher didn't miss it.

When Alistair didn't immediately respond, James spoke again. "Where is the other phone?" he demanded.

Alistair tipped his head back, sighing heavily. "It's in the pipe underneath the left sink in my bathroom."

His eyes remained closed and Asher wondered if his brother didn't want to look at him.

"I'll call you back," James said quickly.

Alistair looked to his feet. "Don't start," he said quietly. "I was out of options and I had no one to turn to."

But Asher shook his head, his expression full of disappointment. "You're wrong. You had options, but your pride got in the way of them."

Alistair's eyes snapped to Asher and his jaw set. "Pride? What the fuck do I have to be prideful about?" His words were short, clipped.

Asher sighed. "You just made some bad choices, Alistair. You're not a bad person . . . and you're capable of much more than you think you are."

His office door swung open and James walked in carrying a phone and bag of white powder.

"Burner phone and a few more days' supply," he said with raised eyebrows.

Alistair only looked away.

"Can you trace the calls?" Asher asked, assuming there were some to trace.

"Samuel is working on it," James said, sounding tired. Then he looked to Alistair, his face hardening. "You should've told me about this phone."

"Why?" Alistair snarked defensively with a weak shake of his head.

"Because two messages arrived yesterday, and that information would've been really fucking helpful," James said, his voice menacing.

Alistair frowned like he'd eaten something sour, and Asher felt dizzy.

"What did the messages say?" Asher asked.

James looked at him with an apology in his eyes, then sighed. "They're a list of addresses and times. They correspond with the attacks."

Asher's jaw fell open. "What?" he asked, his voice a whisper.

James bit his lip. "It's odd, given the messages have come from the same source as other messages that were not so nice. My initial thought was that someone was trying to help you . . . but on second thought, maybe this message was meant as a torment. Maybe they wanted Alistair to see it afterward, when it was too late."

Asher's jaw ground together and he fought the urge to scream. He could've protected the people of Santina—he could've stopped the bombings!"

Asher locked his eyes on his brother's. "What else haven't you told me?"

Alistair's face was an off-white color and he slowly lifted his gaze, looking directly at Asher. "Nothing, I swear. That's the only burner phone I have," he said, then paused. "And the only bag of cocaine I have," he added quietly, sounding tormented.

Asher considered his brother's words for a moment, then looked at James. "Bring Troy in."

James drew a short breath between his teeth and seemed to brace himself. "Troy was seen not far from the restaurant last night. Abi and Rachel saw him, as you would've heard through the communication lines. But he hasn't been seen since the attack. He didn't return home last night and he hasn't used his phone or touched his bank account in days."

Asher paused. "Do you think he's dead?"

James looked thoughtful for a moment. "Perhaps. But if I were going to wager a bet, I'd say he's in hiding. I think we scared him last night and he's taking precautions. But we'll find him, I promise you that." He searched Asher's eyes. "Is there anyone else you've ever heard use the phrase *velvet stamped*? Think carefully."

There was something in James's eyes that gave him pause. Suppressing a chill, Asher reached through his mind, searching through years of memories. "No."

James looked uncertain and Asher didn't understand why.

"What about his father?" James asked.

Asher balked. "My father's brother?"

James nodded unapologetically. "The stakes are high, and when there's power involved, blood ties mean nothing to some people. You wouldn't be the first case I've worked where a family member was behind the attack."

"No," Asher said, but even he heard the uncertainty in his voice. "I mean . . . I don't know. I didn't have much to do with my uncle—he didn't accompany me on any trips and he wasn't an advisor—so I don't know him well enough to know if he's capable of murdering his own brother. But, I suppose he could've said it and that's where Troy picked it up."

James nodded slowly. "Troy will be the focus . . . but I'm not ruling out his father."

ABI

Abi's stomach churned as she watched the television footage of the protestors lining the streets of Santina. Asher was due to make an announcement any minute, and Abi prayed that his words—the truth—would be enough to settle the crowd.

As if the retaliation attacks hadn't been enough, the press had been leaked evidence that Asher had warning of the attack but had chosen to ignore that warning in order to protect Abi. Her teeth ground together at the unfairness of it all. Hadn't Asher been through enough? Hadn't they all?

But then, when was life ever fair?

She sat her coffee down on the table, deciding she didn't need another ounce of caffeine right now. There was enough adrenaline and fury racing through her veins to power the city.

The door swung open and Rachel walked in, security closing it behind her.

"I thought you'd be here, torturing yourself," she said, sitting beside Abi.

"What am I supposed to do? Eat cake and sip on champagne while Asher deals with this mess?" she asked bitterly, shaking her head.

Rachel chewed on her cheek, thoughtful. "If Martin Snider, or

Troy, or whoever it was behind the attacks hadn't used you to get to Asher, they would've used someone else—so you should stop feeling guilty for something that's not your fault."

"Who does Asher have left that they could've targeted? They've tried to take everyone from him," Abi said with a strained voice.

"But they didn't succeed," Rachel said. "I know this is hard for you to watch, but I think you're underestimating Asher right now."

Abi kept her eyes on the television as Asher walked out onto the balcony. The crowd jeered insults and Abi was glad she couldn't make out exactly what they were saying. She hoped Asher couldn't either.

Asher stood tall and calm, giving the crowd a moment to have their say.

"Today is a day of heartbreak for Santina, and one that will torment our kingdom for many years to come. I have spoken to the families of the attacks, but I come here today to give you, and all Santinians, the facts regarding what occurred last night, because what you've been told—conveniently leaked to the press—is so far from the truth it makes my blood boil," Asher said, his voice like a growl.

The crowd quieted.

Asher continued, "It is true that I knew about the attacks several hours in advance, but I did not know the full details of each attack. It is also true that I was advised if I handed over Abigail Bennett, the attacks would not go ahead. But that's the thing about doing business with criminals: they don't stand by their word. The person behind these attacks is the same person who killed my father, your late king. Would you have trusted them?"

The crowd was silent.

"Regardless, a strategy was devised by my security team and Abi. It was not a plan I willingly accepted, but my hands were tied. Abi volunteered to meet the men behind the attacks at a specific location. She put her life at risk, and her life was almost taken. But thanks to an incredibly experienced and skilled security team, Abi survived."

Asher paused, looking directly into the camera. "As a result of her heroic plan, Lamberi—a warlord known for capturing, mutilating, torturing, and raping thousands of women—was killed. Before Abi left last night, she said to me, 'If we can do one thing to make this world a better, safer place, eliminating Lamberi would be it.' Lamberi is the same man who tried to take her hostage a few weeks ago, the same man she told me she wouldn't have survived. So I ask you, if you had been in her position, would you have volunteered to walk back into his reach?"

No one muttered a word.

"I admit," Asher said, shaking his head softly, "I didn't want the plan to go ahead. I've already attended two funerals in as many months, and I couldn't stand the thought of attending a third—or potentially worse: Abi being captured and living the rest of her life in horror. Lamberi and his cohorts have tried to strip everything from me—from Santina. They took your king, tried to kill your queen, and have attempted to ruin my leadership every day since King Martin's assassination."

Asher's eyes darkened. "But now we know exactly who is behind the murders . . . and the attacks last night. Lamberi was involved, but the treason runs much deeper. We were in the darkness, fearing our enemies, but now the tables have turned. Our enemies should be fearing us, because they will pay for the lives of the innocent Santinians they murdered last night!" Asher's voice boomed.

"They will pay, and they will scream for mercy, but we will not give it to them. I will make you one promise, Santina: this is my kingdom, and I will make sure those responsible for last night burn in hell. There will be no mercy. There will be no leniency. I did not forsake Santina last night, and I never will. This ends now!"

The booming cheer of the crowd filled the room and the cameras swept over the thousands of Santinians lining the streets before returning to their king. Asher was a picture of calmness, except for his eyes—his eyes were narrowed, determined, harrowing.

Hail King Asher.

Abi exhaled with relief. If Asher was going to bring down his cousin and cohorts, and ruin Adani, the last thing he needed to worry about was Santina turning on him. But for now, they could all breathe again.

"Not bad," Rachel said with an appreciative smile. "Your man sure knows how to make a killer speech."

Abi nodded. "He cares about people first and foremost—that's why he's so good."

Rachel nodded, and her expression softened. "His life is never going to be fair, Abi. He's going to be criticized—constantly—and harsh accusations will be made against him. And you need to figure out how to deal with that. You're so used to protecting people, but you won't be able to protect him from this."

Abi sighed, rubbing her tired eyes. "I know, it's just hard. I want to take away his pain."

Rachel smiled. "We both know pain can be a good tool. I don't make light of Noah or King Martin's death, but I don't know if Asher would be the same man today without that happening. Whether he does it consciously or not, Asher knows how to use pain to his advantage. If I were his enemies, after today and the speech he gave at his father's funeral, I'd be scared right now."

"They won't stop. They're too far in," Abi said. At this point, there was no turning back for them.

"They don't have to stop," Rachel said. "They just need to be caught."

Abi opened her mouth to respond, but the door swung open and Reed entered. "Good," he said, his eyes landing on them. "Meeting, Asher's office."

He turned and left without another word.

"I mean, I don't care much for small talk, but he needs to work on his delivery a little," Abi mumbled.

Rachel's lips turned up as they followed Reed out.

Abi inhaled deeply, not expecting any good news to come of this, but she followed them regardless.

Asher was in his office when they arrived, and his eyes landed on her the moment she stepped inside. She was caught in his gaze, and it took her a moment to see the photographs on the screen. Abi sucked in a breath. It took her another minute for the location in the background to register.

Rachel's apartment.

Her gaze darted to Rachel, whose skin had turned a greenish tint.

"What . . .?" she asked, her voice hoarse.

"These photographs were taken a few minutes ago," James said. "We received a security breach for your apartment. The security system was disabled, so as yet we don't have any intelligence except for these photographs, which were taken by my crew."

"Who is that?" Rachel's asked, her voice breaking.

Abi's gaze returned to the photographs and she couldn't look away from the woman's platinum-blond hair splayed over the wooden floor boards, the ends dyed red from blood spilled from the woman's slit throat.

"We don't know yet," James finally said.

"I thought you had security on our apartments," Abi said, trying to organize her scrambled thoughts. The words came out sounding more like an accusation than she'd intended.

"We did until last night," James said with a grimace. "I pulled every available man for your meeting with Lamberi and then they went to the bombing sites last night."

"When was she killed?" Abi asked.

"We don't know the exact time, but given the state of her corpse and the forensic evidence, we think she was killed at the apartment around midnight," James aid.

"Why?" Rachel blurted out. "Why my apartment? I don't even know who she is."

"We don't know why they chose your apartment. Are you sure you've never seen her before?" Reed asked as the image on the screen changed, displaying a less gruesome image of who was surely the same woman.

Abi looked to Rachel. "No, but . . ."

"She looks like me," Abi said, swallowing the lump in her throat.

James nodded. "I think it's a message. We're going to report this to the police and provide palace security footage to confirm Rachel has been here with us. That will exclude her from suspicion of murder," he said, looking at Rachel. "From there, I would like to send someone to pack up your apartment because I assume you don't want to go back there . . ." He trailed off questioningly, sounding unsure.

"No," Rachel said resolutely.

James nodded. "I'll find you a more secure apartment," he said, sounding distracted as he looked at his phone. "Excuse me for a moment," he went on before moving toward the door. All eyes followed him, then looked to Reed.

"Okay," Reed said, immediately taking control and looking at Rachel. "Samuel will continue to gather information on this woman."

Rachel nodded, still looking ashen.

"Have you found Troy?" Abi asked. "He's never had to hide before, so I don't expect him to be good at it. Surely he'll make a mistake soon."

"We found him," Reed said, and Abi's eyes snapped to Asher's. He didn't seem surprised by the news. "We have full observation teams on site, but until we can be sure of Alistair's son's location, we're not going to make a move unless forced to do so. If Troy is the person behind these attacks, he's capable of murdering the child without a second thought. We need to play our cards very carefully."

Abi agreed, but that left one major question. "What if he slips away?"

"He won't," Reed said. "We have every door and window under observation."

"Can he go underground?" Abi asked, thinking of the tunnels beneath the palace and the restaurant.

"No. Samuel was able to find the building submissions for the property that he's inside. They had issues laying the foundation because of the granite in the soil, so there won't be any tunnels underneath. He's trapped," Reed said with a menacing smile, "and he doesn't even know it."

ASHER

Silence filled the apartment, and it had never sounded so sweet. He closed the door behind them, followed Abi into the bedroom, then closed the bedroom door too—another barrier between them and the outside world.

Drawing Abi into his arms, he sighed softly. Last night felt like years ago.

She tightened her arms around him, and he placed his lips on the crown of her head.

"How are you?" she asked, tilting her chin up, watching him—perhaps to see if he was going to lie. But he wasn't—his guard was down with Abi. It always had been.

"Tired," he said with a groan.

She gave a small smile. "Santina loved your speech tonight. I loved it."

"It'll hopefully keep the wolves at bay for a few days," Asher said, feeling no satisfaction from his speech. He was angry that Santina was furious with him given how much he'd potentially sacrificed—how much Abi had potentially sacrificed. He knew no one except those involved in the mission would ever understand and he couldn't expect them to—yet he wanted them to. He was trying to do his best in his new role, and he wondered if his best would ever be good enough.

He groaned, rubbing the back of his neck.

Abi raised onto her tiptoes and brushed her lips over his. The tension melted from his body. He groaned softly as she slid his suit jacket off and unbuttoned his shirt. He watched her eagerly, anticipating how far she would take this. His shirt fell to the floor and she kissed his chest. He closed his eyes, reveling in her touch. Her hands moved to his belt and he found it harder to breathe. Last night had been amazing, and yet if felt like a distant memory. So much had happened in the last few hours. Santina had been attacked, he'd discovered the identity of his traitor, and he felt like he finally understood his brother for the first time in years—something he prayed he wasn't mistaken about.

Abi led him to the bed. He slipped off his shoes and laid down, his eyes closing before he could stop them.

"Good to see the effect I have on you," she said with a laugh.

Asher grinned, bolting upright and grabbing her. He fell back onto the bed, pulling her into his arms. She laughed as they bounced on the mattress. "Give me an hour of sleep and I'll fuck you until sunrise."

Abi barked a laugh. "Wow. Asher the *romantic*," she said, giggling.

Asher laughed, tilting her chin to his. "Honestly, if you didn't mean so much to me, I'd rip your clothes off right now. But I don't want to give you only half of me. The other half is absent, reeling, and can hardly think straight."

She propped herself on her elbow and threaded her fingers through his. "I'll wait. You're worth every minute of waiting for."

He ran his thumb over her cheek, locking his gaze on hers. She held his heart captive. "I love you," he whispered. He'd told her as much last night, but that had been in the heat of the moment before she was about to leave and face Lamberi. He'd meant it, meant it as much then as he did now, but he needed her to know it wasn't something he'd said casually.

She searched his eyes. "I love you too. I think you're the strongest man I've ever known, Asher," Abi whispered. "I was scared for you today but I had no reason to worry."

She gave a sad smile. "How did you feel standing on the balcony?"

He sighed. "When the crowd was heckling me?"

Abi nodded.

"Like a failure. I'd never seen that response toward my father. Never. And it took me all of a week to raise it from Santina."

"It was an unfair judgment and very short-lived," Abi reminded him.

"Yeah," he said, looking past her, his mind distracted. "Maybe next time it won't be."

"If you stay true to who you are, you'll always win the people. You proved that today," she said, squeezing his hand.

Now it was his turn to search her eyes. "Do you have any regrets about us? It's been a lot to take in this week."

She answered without hesitation. "No. None," she said, never breaking eye contact. "I'm proud to stand beside you."

He paused. The words were in his throat, and the moment felt so right.

"Stand beside me forever. Marry me, Abi," he said, his weary voice growing stronger.

Her eyes widened. "Are you proposing right now?"

He grinned at her response. "Well, I plan on proposing again, properly. But, yes. I know we haven't been together long but I don't need another minute to know this is a good decision—the best decision I'll ever make. I want you. Forever."

Her eyes glistened. "Yes," she said, her voice a hoarse whisper. "Yes, I'll marry you."

Asher cupped her cheek and pressed his lips to hers, unable to wipe the smile off his face. She parted her lips and his tongue swept over hers, needy and hungry.

He pulled her on top of him as he deepened the kiss. She moaned into his mouth and energy shot through his veins.

She would be his queen.

The Queen of Santina.

They would rule together, and their enemies would fear them.

REED

"*In* position. Target visible," Reed whispered beneath his breath. The blazing Santinian sun had melted into the horizon and now he tugged his jacket around his waist to keep warm.

"*Hold*," James said via his earpiece, followed by a grunt. Reed's gaze swept up to the palm trees but he couldn't make out James's silhouette.

Reed returned his attention to the front window as a shadow darted across. He followed the shadow to the next window and then the corner window. The curtain opened ever so slightly, but Reed didn't miss it.

"Figure at my three o'clock, looking through the window," Reed confirmed. "Should I wave at him?" he asked wryly.

"*Are you sure it's a he?*" Cami asked, entering the conversation.

Reed smirked. "No, Cami, I'm not. Trust me, I wish there were more females like you in this world."

Cami laughed. "*You need someone to calm you down, not encourage you. And someone like me would definitely encourage your bad behavior.*"

"*You're distracting him now, Cami*," James said.

Reed grinned when he heard Cami laugh. "*Yes, boss,*" she said.

"*In position,*" James said. "*Reed, move to position two. I'll cover you.*"

Reed crouched and ran toward the hedge surrounding the front property. From a security point of view, hedges were a terrible idea—especially for a safe house. So, either Troy and his entourage weren't as good as they should be or the information was wrong and tonight would be a bust.

The streetlight beamed over the front garden, but Reed stayed out of its reach, crouching low in the darkness. He paused, listening for any movement.

"Position three," James commanded, and Reed ran for the stairs leading up onto the veranda. He tested the first step and when it didn't creak, he stepped onto the next. None of the stairs creaked—another mistake.

Reed paused at that thought. Troy might be a rookie, but he'd successfully assassinated two people under heavy security protection.

A chill ran down his spine. Something wasn't right about this.

"James, none of the stairs creak. Something doesn't feel right," Reed whispered under his breath.

James paused for a minute. *"Put the robots down. Be careful."*

Reed grabbed six robots from his front pocket and placed them on the decking. Samuel would drive them into position until the front door opened and they could get them inside.

As he placed the last one on the ground, he heard raised voices inside.

He strained to listen, but the voices were muffled.

"It's your fault! Asher should be dead!"

"You said I could trust him. You should be taking the blame!"

Reed held his breath, not daring to move an inch.

He heard the person respond, but couldn't make out what was said. Reed took a step forward, and then another, inching toward the window. He crouched below it, hoping to hear the voices more clearly. Adrenaline rushed through his veins. Something was off; he just didn't know what.

But he didn't get the chance to think about it further, because the front door swung open and a man in uniform stormed out. Reed didn't waste the opportunity. He raised his weapon and caught the door with his foot, sliding inside and into the shadows of the unlit dining room.

He stilled, listening, ready to react.

"I captured a screenshot of his face. Running it through facial recognition now. The team will follow him," Samuel said.

"Reed, confirm position," James said.

"Inside, dining room," Reed whispered so quietly he could barely hear himself.

James swore under his breath, indicating he'd heard, but he didn't order Reed to leave.

And Reed didn't want to leave. He knew for sure there was at least one more person in this house.

Reed took note of the house. He heard a television blaring from one of the back rooms. He lifted his gaze to the ceiling, sweeping it for cameras.

James must've had the same thoughts. *"Reed, you're going to have a few minutes at most. Make them count!"*

Reed moved into the hallway. He scoped the first two rooms but nothing looked out of place.

He moved into the bedroom. The light was off and the room quiet, but an adjoining door was closed and light seeped underneath the door. Reed assumed it was a bathroom, but he couldn't be sure. He paused, listening for a moment, but he didn't hear any movement inside the room. He didn't know if he should scope the rest of the house and come back, or go straight into the bathroom.

"James, light coming from the bathroom adjoining the bedroom closest to the front door. Going in," Reed said. He inched forward carefully, his weapon high, his finger on the trigger, his heart drumming in his chest.

"Be careful," James said, sounding distracted.

"Copy," Reed whispered, his attention focused on the door.

He moved toward the adjoining wall, using it for protection and then pressed his ear to the door.

He could've heard a pin drop.

Silently, carefully, Reed placed his hand on the doorknob and turned it. His body was riled and whoever he met tonight had better be ready for a fight.

He stilled when the door opened to reveal a basin full of empty hair-dye packets and hair clippings.

"James, whoever left out the front door is in disguise!" Reed said quickly, spinning around when he heard footsteps behind him. He ducked as a bullet shattered the mirror behind him.

Reed dove for the shooter's legs, knocking him to the floor.

A boot slammed into the side of his face, startling him for a second. Before he knew it, he was pinned on the ground. But that gave him one advantage: he had a clear view of the man's face.

"Captain Lewis Spencer," Reed said, knowing the team would hear him.

The man smiled widely, but Reed quickly wiped that off his face.

Reed brought his knee up, grabbed his knife and slammed it into the captain's shoulder. He roared, loosening his grip on Reed, and that was all he needed. Reed rolled out of the man's grip before he had a chance to correct his mistake, then lunged at the captain, grabbing his jaw and snapping his head back. He held his knife at the man's jugular and grinned.

Checkmate.

"Where's Troy?"

The captain blinked, seemingly surprised. "I . . . don't . . . know," he hissed.

Reed pushed the tip of the knife against his skin, careful not to break through. He didn't actually want to kill him—not yet at least.

"We don't know. He disappeared last night . . . called us today . . ." the captain went on.

"Where's your phone?" Reed asked.

"Back . . . pocket."

Reed grabbed a syringe from his own back pocket and jammed it into the man's neck. The captain exhaled, resigned, and went limp. Reed dropped him on the floor.

Reed searched his back pocket and found the phone. It was locked, but Reed knew the captain would open it for them when he awoke—Reed would make sure of it.

He slipped the phone into his pocket and moved back into the hallway. He doubted anyone else was inside. If they were, they would've come running at the sound of the gunshot.

Nonetheless, he was careful, scoping the house like he would any other. He paused at a locked door. Picking the lock, he carefully opened it only to find that he needn't have worried.

She was slumped against the wall, her eyes rolled back, her mouth foaming. He ran toward her and placed two fingers on her wrist. No pulse.

She was cold, and it didn't take him long to determine the cause of death.

"James, I found Alistair's . . . fling. No pulse. Suspected opioid overdose," he said as his eyes landed on a syringe on the ground not far from her hand.

"Damn!" James swore under his breath. *"I wanted her alive."*

ASHER

*A*sher stood in front of the glass, his eyes never leaving Captain Spencer. James sat opposite him, and Reed lingered behind the captain.

The captain was just waking up, and he'd woken up in hell. Asher prayed he never woke up with men like Reed and James looking at him like he was dinner.

James slapped the captain, who jolted, pressing back against the chair. Reed laid his hands on the man's shoulders, and it was only then that Captain Lewis Spencer really understood how much danger he was in.

"What do you want?" he asked quickly, his voice thick and groggy.

"I want you to tell me everything you know. It's going to be a long story, and I have all night," James said, his voice impossibly cold. It almost didn't sound human. Asher wondered if he'd practiced that voice in front of the mirror . . . or if it had developed purely through repetition. Asher shuddered at the thought.

"Who was at the house with you?" Reed asked, running a blade over the captain's neck as if he were shaving him.

The captain's teeth ground together, but he was smart enough to realize he had no choice but to talk.

"My brother," he said, more quickly than Asher expected. Samuel had already confirmed it was his brother, but it was interesting how easily the captain gave him up. If his loyalty to his brother was so shallow, how far did his loyalty to Troy extend?

For the first time tonight, Asher felt hopeful.

"Who took Colonel Stevens from his house?" James asked, surprising Asher.

"I didn't do it alone," he said quickly.

"That's not what I asked," James said, leaning forward. He had something in his hands, but Asher couldn't see it from where he stood.

The captain's eyes dropped to James's, and then he quickly said, "We did. Me, my brother, Troy, and a few others."

"Why did you keep him alive?"

"Because we didn't think he was giving us the truth. We thought he'd reported us to Asher," the captain said.

"You were wrong," James said.

Asher looked at James carefully—another surprise.

The captain's eyebrows lifted. "Huh."

"Last night you said Troy left and you could only contact him by phone. What happened?" James asked.

"Why are you so interested in Troy?" the captain asked.

James slammed an instrument—what Asher thought looked like a scalpel—into the man's leg. The captain howled, rocking against the chair, but Reed didn't let it fall. He held his knife to the captain's neck, unflinching—nothing about James's tactics surprised him nor made him uncomfortable.

Asher, on the other hand, felt a little ill as he watched blood drip from the man's leg, pooling on the floor.

"I ask the questions!" James said sharply, his voice like a blade slicing the air.

"I don't know, he just said he had to go and to only contact him via phone! Martin's losing control and Troy's his right-hand man," the captain blurted.

Asher narrowed his eyes. Did Asher have it wrong, or did the captain not know who Martin Snider was?

"Everyone hailed Martin, but after Lamberi died, whispers of doubt formed," the captain whispered. "Martin has been planning this revolution for years. He'd convinced his men—his followers—that King Martin wasn't strong enough to lead. When the succession changed, he turned them against Asher." He glanced at Asher for a second before returning to James. "But Asher's proving him wrong, and Martin's hold is weakening. Hell, even I would back Asher after last night. Asher's different than his father: stronger, and more willing to take a stand against our rivals. That's what we all want—what Santina wants."

"To take a stand against your rivals?" James asked casually. Asher wondered if he didn't buy the captain's praise of Asher, and Asher wondered if he should believe a word that the captain was saying himself. He did have a knife to his neck, and another in his leg; he would surely say anything that he thought might save him.

"Adani," the captain said, like it was the most obvious thing in the world.

"Your little revolution is being *aided* by Adani," James said, crossing his arms.

The captain nodded carefully, highly aware of the knife at his throat. "The plan was to turn around and blame them. Then we would take Adani too."

James was quiet a moment and Asher wanted—for a split second—to get inside his mind.

"And how would you have personally benefitted from this?" James asked.

"Martin said I'd be made Commander in Chief," he said with a touch of pride that made Asher's teeth clench.

"He would never have given you that role," James said, sounding amused.

The captain jutted his jaw as his eyes narrowed. "What makes you so sure of that?"

"Because he'll use you just like he's using everyone else. A man like

Martin Snider is only looking out for one person: Martin Snider. Don't be fooled, Lewis . . . you're a pawn in his game just as much as anyone," James said, like he knew Martin Snider himself. On some level, Asher supposed he did; he'd likely dealt with men like him most of his life.

The captain was quiet, thoughtful, and it was only then that he realized James's game plan. The corner of Asher's lips turned up. *Let's see how this plays out.*

"Have you ever met Martin?" James asked.

"No one has," he responded.

James shook his head. "Not true. Lamberi did. Do you know why he was able to meet him? Because Lamberi demanded more respect from Martin—and if he was going to do a deal with Martin, he wanted to see his face."

The captain didn't respond, but Asher could sense he was rattled. He had obviously considered himself at the top of Martin's food chain, and that Martin had made a different deal with Lamberi challenged that idea.

"So you know who Martin is?" the captain finally asked.

"Of course we do," James responded without hesitation, his voice void of arrogance. It was simply a statement.

"What do you want from me?" the captain asked.

Asher nodded his head, knowing James must be equally pleased.

"Lead us to him," James said.

"And you'll protect me?" the captain asked.

"That will depend on your loyalty to King Asher," James said coolly. "And that will be Asher's choice to make."

He paused, then leaned in slowly toward the captain, his eyes full of danger. "But if you so much as breathe in the wrong direction, I will slit your throat faster than you can plead for mercy."

The captain visibly swallowed.

Asher refrained from grinning like a maniac.

"Don't move," James said with a hint of humor before he left the room. James closed the door and strode toward Asher.

"Thoughts?" James asked, yet again surprising Asher. He wondered how many times in one day this man could surprise him.

"He broke easily," Asher said.

James nodded. "That's what happens when you don't put a face to a name. The ties are weak, and when someone has a knife to your throat, you'll give them up in a second."

"Is it a good idea to use him?" Asher asked.

"Yes, if we play it carefully. I need a few hours to think about the strategy, but essentially I think the captain should demand a face-to-face meeting with Martin Snider. He can say that things are too hot right now and he refuses to talk on the phone. Martin—Troy—might not agree, but he might say something we can use. I think we should do it."

"Okay." Asher nodded, and then his eyes went hard. "Please tell me this plan doesn't involve Abi."

"No, she's done her part and Lamberi is dead. I won't put her in harm's way again, you have my word," James said.

Asher searched his eyes, but he needn't have—the conviction in James's voice was promise enough, and Asher already knew James's word was as good as ink. As Asher's father had always said to him, *"Do business with honest people—people you can do a handshake deal with. If you can't do a handshake deal, don't work with them."*

For people like James and Asher, integrity was everything. If you couldn't stand by your word, what could you stand by?

ABI

Abi paused when she heard a familiar voice. She began to turn around, but Emilia stopped her. "Abi!"

Abi's eyes widened. "I'm sorry, I didn't realize you were out here. I'm sorry for interrupting," she said quickly.

"Not at all," Emilia said as she walked toward Abi, her long gown trailing on the soft grass. Her assistant went in the other direction. "These gardens have always been my favorite place to clear my mind."

"They're beautiful," Abi said quietly, looking over them.

"They are. My children used to play hide and seek in these gardens for hours," she said with a sad smile. "All of them together—Alistair, Asher. and Noah."

Abi hid her surprise. She knew that the brothers had grown apart, but she couldn't imagine them as friends—even as children.

"It seems Asher was quite fond of hide and seek. He told me he would play that in the tunnels too," Abi said.

Emilia smiled properly, her eyes lighting up. "I could never find my children," she said with a laugh. "Things were much simpler then. How is he today?" she asked, then quickly added, "I spoke to him earlier, but Asher has a good poker face. Sometimes it's hard for me to really know what's going on inside his head."

"He said you can read him better than anyone." Abi smiled, remembering how Asher had told her his mother was the first to know of their relationship. "But, honestly, I think he's doing well, all things considered. At moments I feel like it's not fair—the role he needs to play—but I also think he's doing an amazing job."

Emilia nodded, understanding. "I would often think that when I looked at Martin. And I used to fear that—and still do—for my children." She looked at Abi, her eyes far away. "I don't know how much Asher or your father told you, but before the affair happened, I lost a child."

Abi put her hand on her chest. "I'm sorry, I didn't know."

Emilia shook her head. "I felt like a failure, but in all honestly, there was one tiny, tiny part of me that was relieved. Relieved that I wouldn't burden my child with the responsibility I knew weighed so heavily on my husband's shoulders. And then I felt guilty for feeling like that too, which spiraled things out of control." She sighed heavily. "But here's what I've learned, Abi. Challenges only make us stronger. We are never given more than we can handle—even if we don't think we can handle it, we can. And I tell myself that every morning now. Asher will rise up. I know he will. His role is one of great responsibility, and it is also one of great privilege." She looked to her right, her gaze sweeping over the blushing rose gardens. "Walk with me," she said with a nod.

"Of course," Abi said, falling into step beside Emilia, her future mother-in-law. She thought over Asher's clearly unplanned proposal and smiled. Nothing he did was conventional, and she was beginning to learn that was one of the things she loved most about him.

"Did you read the papers this morning?" Emilia asked, looking ahead.

"I did."

Emilia looked to her, smiling.

"You're being heralded as a hero, and quite rightly. Leaking our own intelligence to the media was a good move," she said with a knowing grin. "Asher told me all about what happened last night and how you gave him no choice. I liked you even more when I heard."

Abi blushed.

"Asher has waited his whole life to meet someone like you. I was always trying to introduce him to someone, but no one held his interest for more than a few seconds. That's how I knew, actually," she said with a big smile. "Asher looked your way more than once at that charity dinner, and I'd never seen him do that." She laughed softly. "I'm glad he found you, Abi. I mean that."

"Thank you," Abi said as a white butterfly flew past her.

Her gaze followed it, almost jumping when her eyes landed on Alistair. He stood in the shadows of the palace, appearing to watch them. He didn't look away.

What was he doing?

Her heart raced a little faster. She couldn't see security, but she knew they were around—both she and Emilia had teams following them everywhere.

Alistair smiled, but there was something in his eyes she didn't like, and she suppressed a shiver as he strode toward them.

"Abigail," he said as he approached them.

"Hello, Alistair," she said, keeping her voice neutral.

She looked to Emilia, who seemed happy to see her eldest son.

"Thank you for the chat, Emilia. I'll leave you two to catch up," Abi said before turning away. As she took a step forward, security emerged to escort her away but she couldn't help feeling like eyes were boring into her back.

It was unsettling and she questioned if she was imaging things. Alistair's involvement had been explained, hadn't it?

Admittedly, he'd also made it very clear he didn't like Abi. Was he jealous?

How stable was Alistair?

"Where is Asher?" she asked the guard beside her.

"In his office. He's in the middle of a strategic meeting," he responded.

Abi nodded. "Okay. I'll go to my office," she said, glad she'd spent the morning setting up the office Asher had given her.

The palace was quiet as they walked the hallways. She entered her office and closed the door behind her, knowing security would stand at her door.

She glanced around, turned on her computer, and began research work of a different type.

ASHER

Asher's foot tapped mercilessly as he watched the security cameras.

James Thomas walked into the cell and sat opposite Captain Lewis Spencer, who lifted his eyes to meet James's. Asher noted the dark shadows beneath his eyes and the lines that seemed permanently creased into his forehead. The man looked like he'd aged ten years in ten hours.

"You're going to call Troy and tell him you were captured by us. The house you had was under surveillance, so there's no point lying about it. Tell him you were captured and you made a deal with us to be released." James slid a piece of paper across the table then continued, "Tell him you've spoken to Martin Snider and you're going to meet him. Tell him you're sorry about last night and that you'll sort this mess out."

The captain's eyebrows threaded together. "But he knows I don't know who Martin Snider is."

"Does he know that for sure?" James asked simply.

Silence hung in the air.

James folded his hands on the table. "If he asks where you're meeting him, give him the address on this piece of paper."

"And then what?" the captain asked.

"Then you're going to attend the meeting and you're going to do everything I tell you to do. One wrong move and I will put a bullet between your eyes before you can take another breath."

Asher bit his lip, watching the captain's response closely. He visibly swallowed, took a breath, and then straightened his shoulders. "Okay," he said, his voice strained.

James slid a phone across the table and the captain picked it up with trembling hands. James nodded and the call was made.

Asher heard the call connect and realized Samuel was broadcasting the call in his office. The phone continued to ring, and just when Asher thought it was going to ring out, he heard the familiar voice.

"Hello," Troy said.

"Hey," the captain said. "I'm in trouble. They found us last night—Asher's guys," he said quickly, on the verge of rambling. "I'm sorry, I had no choice, Troy. They let me go, but I had to give them something in return . . ."

"What did you give them?" Troy asked, the tone of his voice shifting. Asher's eyes narrowed instinctively.

"I had no choice!" the captain said desperately, glancing nervously at James. "I had no choice. I'm giving them Martin Snider."

A long pause followed. Asher didn't breathe, he didn't move. He looked to James, but his face was impassive. A picture of calm.

"How do you know who Martin Snider is?" he asked. Asher didn't like the tone of his voice, and judging by the way he looked to James, Asher didn't think the captain liked it either.

"The things I've heard. The phone calls I've traced," the captain said vaguely. "I've set a trap for him. We don't need him. We can lead this revolt without him. He's never bothered to meet us anyway! What do we need him for?"

Asher studied the captain now—his voice surprisingly convincing. Maybe those words weren't an act.

"You have no idea what you're talking about!" Troy said, his words biting. "What trap have you set?"

"I'm going to meet him. I gave him an address and told him to meet me there."

"You fool," Troy hissed. "Give me that address!"

James nodded and the captain reeled off the address from the piece of paper. Asher feared it might sound like he was reading it, but it didn't. There was a genuine tremble and fluster to the captain's voice that made it believable.

"If you do this, you'll end up dead. If Martin doesn't kill you, Asher's guys will. You betrayed the king—you're good for nothing now, and Asher won't pardon you."

"I had no choice," the captain said simply.

Silence. Then Troy said, "I'll protect you. Don't lead them to Snider. Meet me at Victoria Square, in the train station. They'll kill you, regardless of what they told you. Asher can't be trusted. Nor can James Thomas. Meet me there in two hours. Make sure no one follows you."

"Thank you," the captain said quickly. "I'll see you soon."

The call ended and James stood, nodded, and exited the room. The captain's gaze followed him, looking unsure.

Asher gave James a questioning look as he walked toward him.

"Perfect," James said without explanation.

"Perfect?" Asher repeated, and then the pieces fell into place. "You wanted him to give an alternative address, didn't you? You never intended to use that address."

"Correct. I don't think Troy will reveal himself at the train station either—he's not that stupid—but he'll be there, watching from the shadows. And we'll be in the shadows behind him," James said with a haunting grin. "He chose the train station because it's busy. That creates some concern regarding innocent casualties, but if we play our cards right, this could be a perfect storm."

Asher sighed, tilting his head back and looking at the ceiling. He had to authorize this, and if his security detail was linked to this and innocent Santinians were hurt, he would be responsible for it. Their deaths would be his fault.

"This is our best opportunity because it's a chance to draw Troy out. He's hiding the child somewhere, and while he's busy dealing with us, he won't have time to instruct the babysitter to do anything to harm him. That keeps the boy safe and gives us a chance to take Troy down," James said.

"And if you're seen to be involved in this, and innocent people are killed, what will I say to the media?" Asher asked, his tone sharper than intended. He was beginning to learn that when James said, *"This is our best opportunity,"* he wasn't going to like whatever followed.

"The truth: that the men behind the attacks were at the train station and you were trying to protect further attacks from taking place and more innocent people being harmed," James said, so convincingly Asher almost believed it himself. It was a branch of the truth.

Asher leaned forward, sighing deeply and running his hands over his face.

"Take this opportunity, Asher. You don't always get a second chance," James said, his voice somber.

Asher knew he was right, and he'd already made up his mind.

"Do it," Asher said. He saw the change in James's eyes instantly—it was like Asher had flipped a switch.

James pulled his phone from his pocket and made one call after another. First to Samuel, then Reed, and then to various teams. Within five minutes, everyone had been briefed and the teams assembled.

"Are you planning to watch?" James asked, finally turning back to Asher.

"Yes," Asher said. He couldn't help them in these situations, but he would never be the kind of person who sat in his office, oblivious to what was going on.

"This one will be easier to watch," James said, and Asher nodded in understanding—Abi wasn't involved this time.

"I need to make some final arrangements and suit up. Samuel will hook you up. We'll get this son of a bitch," James said with steely eyes.

"Bring him to me," Asher said. He would not be weak because Troy was his blood; Troy hadn't cared about that when he'd killed Noah or Asher's father. There would be no mercy.

James nodded—a promise, Asher knew—and then turned away. Asher took one last look at Captain Lewis Spencer and wondered if he'd make it out alive. If he didn't, it would be one less problem for Asher to deal with, and it would give Colonel Stevens justice. As harsh as it might be, he wanted that—it would be the king's final gift to the colonel.

Asher went to his office with his security team trailing behind. They closed the door behind him and turned on the screen on the wall while Asher sat at his desk. The towers of mail were multiplying, so much so it looked like a small city was forming on his desk. He needed a few hours of uninterrupted time to go through it all, but everyday there seemed to be a new crisis that stole his attention.

He drew a long, calming breath and looked at his father's crystal clock. It was odd how such a commonplace object could give him so much peace.

What would you do, Father?

Asher stared at the clock as if it would speak to him. He mindlessly rubbed his jaw, thinking through every possibility and analyzing every outcome.

When a knock at his door stole his attention, he looked up into Abi's eyes.

"Hey," she said with a smile.

"Hey, take a seat," Asher said, gesturing to the chair opposite his desk.

Her eyes landed on the towers of mail. "I know things have been crazy, but are you purposely avoiding that?" She sat down, and a memory flashed in his mind of his mother and father in this exact setting.

He looked at her for a moment, then shrugged. "I haven't had a chance to even open it."

Her eyes lingered on it. "Do you want me to open it and sort it for you? I won't read it all," she added quickly.

"Abi," Asher said gently, "you're going to be my partner in this;

you're going to be queen. There's nothing in this office you can't know about—there's nothing I don't want you to know about."

She searched his eyes and he wondered if she thought he was lying or putting on some kind of front. But when she smiled with warm eyes, his doubts vanished.

She picked up a delicately balancing envelope and slid her finger underneath the seal. Asher opened his drawer and found a letter opener—five of them. He suddenly wondered why his father had so many. Was it something he'd collected? Asher picked them up, turning them over. There were no inscriptions nor any symbols or badges that looked familiar to him. He shrugged and passed Abi one.

Together they opened envelope after envelope, sorting them into piles specific to what action Asher needed to take. He needed to send some thank-you notes; reports were collated and general mail was set aside for Asher to delegate to various administrative staff.

They were almost done with the mail when footage flashed up on the screen and the speakers in his office activated.

"What's going on?" Abi asked, turning to look at the screen behind her.

"They've set a trap for Troy," Asher said.

"At the train station?" she asked warily.

"Troy's choice," Asher said, just as Captain Lewis Spencer walked into view.

Abi's eyes went wide. "That's the colonel's driver!"

Asher had forgotten she hadn't been updated on the events of the last few hours. He quickly filled her in.

She stood and dragged her chair around to sit beside Asher so she could watch the screen properly. "Do they know who messaged the bombing times and locations to Alistair's phone?"

"No. The message was sent from an untraceable phone. There's no leads on it at all. Hopefully they'll make contact again soon—with better news," Asher added quickly.

"Hmm," Abi said absently, her eyes on the screen.

Asher looked to see what had stolen her attention.

The captain had stopped to talk to someone—who, Asher didn't know.

"Samuel, do you have sound on him?" Asher asked, aware that when the speaker system was activated, the communications were two-way.

"Yes, I have sound on all feeds and a team member is listening to each one. The captain is asking about the man's family. Nothing of concern. I'm running facial-recognition software on him now, but he doesn't appear to be a threat. Judging by the conversation, I think he's military and they might've worked together in the past."

"Thanks," Asher said, nodding.

The captain shook the man's hand and moved on, continuing toward the marble statue of Asher's grandfather. His eyes remained on the footage, and in the background he saw his own picture framed on the wall. It was customary for photographs of three successions to be framed and displayed in various locations around Santina—usually public places like the train station, hotels, or Town Hall—but it was the first time Asher had actually seen it. He supposed Alistair's photograph had been replaced with his own after the coronation service, but he hadn't given it a thought until now.

He shook his head, clearing his mind. His eyes scanned the background of the footage streams; he didn't see a single one of James's men. But he knew they were there, hiding in the shadows, waiting for an opportunity to strike.

The captain reached the statue and Asher realized his own grip had tightened on his armrests. It was peak hour at the station, which meant it was a sea of rushing civilians. Asher said a quick prayer for them and for James's team.

His eyes continued to scan the passing faces but no one looked familiar. The captain looked around, his eyes darting from point to point. Asher's eyes dropped to the clock and he noted the time.

A minute passed.

Two minutes passed.

The captain looked increasingly nervous, reflecting Asher's inner state.

Where was Troy?

Was it all a setup?

Suddenly, the captain recoiled—a bullet landing between his eyes. Asher's eyes went wide and he gasped as the captain fell. It only took a moment for the crowd around the now dead man to realize what had happened.

Asher's veins turned to ice as he watched the chaos that came next.

Women, men, and children began screaming and running in all directions. Asher couldn't hear their screams, but he felt them.

One brave woman rushed to the captain's side, but she only took one look at him before deciding there was nothing she could do to help him.

She stood, looking like she was about to run—but she never got the chance.

Two bullets landed in her chest and she fell to the floor. Fury blazed in Asher's chest.

REED

Reed pushed through the sea of people, his eyes on the man no more than ten meters in front of him. Troy was wearing a navy-blue sweater and jeans—easily blending into the crowd. But Reed's eyes never left him, and when Reed had a target in sight, it didn't end well for his target.

As James had predicted, Troy wouldn't do the work himself but he'd be there to make sure things went to plan. Admittedly, they hadn't expected Troy to put a bullet between the captain's eyes, but as far as Thomas Security was concerned, that was no huge loss. They'd extracted what information they could from him, and now he'd served his purpose.

Another shot fired somewhere behind Reed and frantic hands pushed into his back as a new wave of fear swept through the crowd. People began falling, concerned only for their own survival.

Reed kept his eyes on his target, even when he tripped. He didn't look down; he didn't look behind him. He had one focus, and one focus only.

"Reed, I'm covering you. Get him!" James commanded via his earpiece.

"Copy. Working on it," Reed said, quickening his pace to keep up with Troy.

Reed wondered if Troy knew they were following him—if Troy sensed eyes on his back. His question was answered when Troy looked over his shoulder, straight at Reed.

Troy's eyes narrowed and he darted to the left, crouching low.

Reed lost sight of him and his pulse accelerated as another gunshot fired and the crowd surged forward, sweeping him farther away from Troy.

"Where are those shots coming from?" Reed asked, fighting against the crowd. "I can't see him! I can't see him!"

"There's a door to your left," Samuel broke in. *"It's his only chance of exiting without going through the front doors of the station."*

It was a risk, but right now it seemed like the only option Reed had. He pushed in that direction but it was a challenge just to keep himself upright in this frantic, panicked sea of people. Hands pushed into him and fingers grabbed onto his shirt as people fought to stay upright and avoid being trampled. Even if no more shots were fired, Reed knew there would be casualties from the stampede. That fueled his determination: if innocent people were going to die, he'd make sure their deaths counted for something—and capturing the king's slayer was something Santina wanted.

Reed's eyes narrowed as a head popped up. He couldn't confirm it was Troy, but he seemed to be looking for something.

The door.

Samuel, you genius.

Reed was almost there. A few more minutes and he'd reach the door.

"A stairwell. He's inside!" Samuel said.

Reed rushed forward but he'd only taken a few steps when he felt the unmistakable sensation of metal against his neck.

He didn't give his attacker a chance to slit his throat.

Reed's elbow came up, slamming beneath his attacker's jaw. Reed hissed as the blade scraped his skin before it fell to the ground. Reed swung around, ducking as a fist came fast at his face. Reed blocked it and returned the favor, landing a hit in the man's throat. The man recoiled, gasping for air and losing his footing. The crowd knocked him to the floor and stepped right over him; Reed knew they'd finish the job.

He turned and ran. It had been a minute or more since Troy entered the stairwell, and that was a minute too many.

Reed pushed through the crowd, desperate. Adrenaline raced through his body, heightening his senses. He reached the door, raised his weapon and kicked it open. Reed stepped into the silence, a sharp contrast from the panicked cries of the crowded station.

The door closed behind him, echoing through the stairwell. He paused, listening, taking a moment to breathe.

He looked up and down.

"Samuel, what's on the rooftop?" Reed asked.

"Helicopter pad!" Samuel responded in a rush.

Reed's foot was on the step when he heard movement below. He paused, not daring to breathe as he strained to hear below. The stairwell was silent. Had he imagined it?

He looked down again but saw nothing.

If he made the wrong call now, it might take them months to find Troy again, and Reed knew there would be retaliation attacks for today. Troy would punish Asher for this—there was no doubt.

Reed looked up again.

He'd wasted too much time.

It made sense Troy would have an escape plan, and a helicopter pad was a good one... but his gut screamed for him to go down.

The pressure of the decision threatened to paralyze him, but Reed had been trained for those exact moments. He stepped back and whispered, "I'm going down!"

He ran down the stairs so fast he felt like he was flying. He was halfway to the bottom and questioning his decision when he heard footsteps echoing below. He surged ahead and saw a flash of Troy over the balustrade, but he wasn't close enough to catch him.

His heart stammered in his chest. He couldn't fail—he hated to lose.

Reed looked to the ground, quickly calculating how many levels up he was, then put his hand on the railing and launched his body over. That was one decision he really hadn't thought through properly. Troy stepped toward the door as Reed came flying down from above. Troy turned, his eyes doubling in size as he raised his weapon.

But Reed flew down like a ninja and knocked the weapon from his hands before landing on the floor in a crouch. He grunted, the wind knocked from his lungs. Pain shot through his feet, all the way to his hips, but he pushed up just in time to block a blow from Troy. The guy was bigger than Reed, and someone had taught him how to fight, at least passably.

The blows kept coming, and there was a fire in Troy's eyes that made the hairs on Reed's neck stand up. It was a look he had seen before: the look of a man prepared to survive at any cost.

Reed ducked, swinging low, balling his fingers into a fist. He landed one in Troy's stomach but it wasn't hard enough. Troy had caught his hand and threw him into the wall. What Troy lacked in technique he was making up for in brute strength.

Reed's head slammed into the wall and he blinked a few times as his vision blurred. But when Troy's fist came at him, he was quick enough to block it. Reed used the block to his advantage, grabbed his weapon, and fired a shot into Troy's shoulder. Blood sprayed and he took a step back, but it didn't stop him.

If Reed could just kill him, this fight would've been over a long time ago—but until they had Alistair's son, that wasn't an option.

"Reed? Reed?" James voice came through urgent.

"Copy," Reed said with a grunt as he defended another blow. Reed needed more space to move, but the cramped stairwell didn't allow for it. Reed crouched and then rushed at Troy, slamming a fist into his injured arm then hitting him twice in the face.

Troy landed a hit, and Reed hissed when it felt like the thin skin of his cheek split. When he tasted blood a second later, he guessed he was right.

"Big mistake," Reed said. Despite his line of work, he was still vain and didn't want a scar on his cheek.

Anger surged through him and he launched up, flying through the air, catching a breathless, pain-riddled Troy unprepared. Reed brought his fist down on Troy's bloody shoulder and slammed his knee into his stomach, knocking the wind from his lungs.

But Reed didn't stop. Instead, he unleashed. He delivered blow after blow, hitting Troy like he was a boxing bag. Blood sprayed from every orifice of Troy's face and only when his eyes rolled back into his head did Reed stop.

Troy's legs buckled first and he slumped to the floor.

A set of footsteps thundered above him and Reed gritted his teeth—but when a familiar face came barreling down the stairs, he lowered his weapon.

James leaned over to look at Troy, then raised his eyebrows. "Please tell me he's going to be able to speak with that broken jaw," he said dryly.

Reed shrugged. "His fingers are fine. He can type."

James smirked. "Let's tie him up and get out of here. It's chaos out there."

ASHER

*A*sher sat across from his once-trusted cousin. Troy's eyelids fluttered, but he had yet to fully wake up.

"He might be out for a while. Reed did quite the number on him," James said.

"I'll wait," Asher said, his voice tight. His throat felt like it was closing in. He was looking at a man he had called a friend . . . and now a man who had murdered his brother and father, attempted to murder his mother, and almost certainly aided in Abi's kidnapping.

Asher would wait.

He wanted to be there the moment Troy opened his eyes.

Minutes passed and James sat beside him, silent. They both knew that what happened next would change Asher's life forever. He would never be the same man—the same person.

"Did you think they would kill the captain like that?" Asher finally asked.

A beat passed. "Not quite like that," James admitted. "They were quick to put a bullet between his eyes. My team was well hidden and I'm certain they didn't see anyone following him. I think Troy issued the order to kill him before the captain ever set foot inside that station. There was never a plan to protect him."

"How do you know who you can trust?" Asher asked, watching James carefully. "How do you know the men you're employing can be trusted?"

"Personally, I keep a very small circle, so that narrows the risk," James said. "And that circle is composed of people I know would die for me. There's very little risk that someone willing to die for you would also betray you." He sighed. "In regards to my staff, I have a very strict policy in place . . . an uncomplicated HR policy," he said without a trace of humor. "If they betray us, we'll kill them—and every staff member knows it. It's an extreme policy, but a necessary one."

"Have you ever had to enforce that policy?" Asher asked carefully, returning his attention to Troy.

"Yes. Not that long ago, unfortunately," James said, with another sigh.

Asher looked at him sidelong. "Do you ever regret it?"

James looked at him with hard eyes. "No. And you won't, either."

Asher looked away, nodding. Noah deserved justice, as did his father.

Troy spluttered a cough and shifted in the chair he was bound to but his eyes remained closed.

James leaned forward and slapped his cheek.

Troy's eyes sprung open and it seemed to take him a few moments to focus. His eyes locked on Asher.

Troy opened his mouth to speak and winced. He rocked forward, as if trying to relieve his pain. But his pain was just beginning.

He opened his mouth gently, managing to speak this time.

"Your . . . Majesty," he said, mockingly.

"You're such a disappointment," Asher said, his voice dripping with contempt. "Why did you do it? Power? Money? Why?" he demanded, his voice rising.

Troy looked like he was trying to smile.

"Your . . . family . . . incompetent," he said, coughing. Blood dribbled down his chin.

Asher's eyebrows lifted and his teeth ground together. His father wasn't incompetent, and he refused to be—but he pushed those feelings aside for the moment.

"Why Noah?" Asher asked.

Troy raised an eyebrow. "Because he was smarter than all of you," he said with hard eyes. "He came to me concerned about whispers of a revolt. He didn't want to worry you, and he didn't think you could do anything about it—so he came to me instead. He wanted me to help shut it down."

Troy scoffed and Asher wanted to smash his fist into Troy's nose.

"I said I'd work on it," Troy continued. "But Noah wasn't stupid, and he had me followed. Did you know that? His mistake was thinking he was untouchable because of you. He thought Jesse would protect him."

"You organized the switch of the meds in his IV bag, didn't you?"

"It was so easy," Troy said with an arrogant smile.

Asher lunged forward, but James had a grip on him before he could raise his fist.

Troy laughed. "Your Majesty, look at you now! This role will break you before you're a few years in. Your father had one thing that you don't: resilience."

Asher grit his teeth. "I'm going to kill you. You will pay for their deaths."

"You can't stop it. You're too late. The wheels are in motion, and it's only a matter of time. And if you kill me, you'll never find that boy," he said with a knowing smile. "If the babysitter doesn't hear from me within the next twenty-four hours, the boy won't live to see the next sunrise. Of all the gifts Alistair gave me, that screaming little thing is the best. I couldn't have asked for better leverage."

"You're going to tell us where he is," James said beside him. His voice was cool, calculated.

Troy looked at him for the first time.

"I'm not weak like the others—like the captain. You can't make me talk," Troy said, lifting his chin to regard James coolly.

Asher looked to James, whose lips turned up.

"I can make anyone talk," James said flatly.

Asher looked back to Troy, who smiled. "The thing is, I just need to hold out for twenty-four hours, and then it won't matter. The boy will be dead, and I'll die a happy man."

James stood with a scalpel in his hand. Asher didn't even know where he'd gotten that from. Had it been up his sleeve or had he been holding it the entire time?

James Thomas—the deadly magician.

James walked around Troy, stopping to stand behind him. For the first time since Troy had opened his eyes, his confidence wavered.

"King Asher," James said, placing his hands on Troy's shoulders. Troy jumped.

James continued. "Here's your first lesson of the day. I'm going to teach you the fastest way to remove someone's face. The ability to skin someone alive is a tool all men should have, don't you think?"

Troy's pupils dilated and Asher would've smiled, except that he couldn't forget—despite it all—that the man sitting in the chair opposite had once been his confidant.

His cousin.

His blood.

James pressed his scalpel to Troy's forehead and sliced from the center of his forehead to his earlobe.

"Step one," James said, his voice chillingly cold. "Slice the skin from forehead to chin." His scalpel continued tracing Troy's jaw, stopping at his chin.

Troy hissed, breathing heavily. Asher's stomach rolled and he wasn't sure he had the stomach for this, but James Thomas seemed to be in his element—his eyes danced with excitement.

"How are you feeling?" James asked, leaning over Troy. He asked the question so pleasantly is was almost comedic.

"Fuck you!" Troy spat.

"Very well," James said, straightening. "Asher, step two: repeat on the other side."

Troy groaned and hissed, bucking against his restraints, swearing obscenities Asher was sure he'd never heard before.

"Step three is where things really become fun," James said with what appeared to be a genuine smile. "It's a little tricky and it takes some practice, but luckily I've had a lot of it." James reached an arm around each side of Troy. "The trick is to get your fingers underneath the thin skin of the chin. And then you slowly peel up, like peeling a thin layer of onion. Don't go too fast, otherwise the skin will rip."

James touched Troy's chin, feeling along the cut lines. Troy screamed, bucking and hissing. Asher's stomach clenched but he didn't make a move to stop James.

"Ready to talk, Troy? I can peel one inch of skin for the next twenty-four hours . . . and you still think you can survive me?"

"Fuck you!" Troy screamed, livid.

James shrugged casually. "On the count of three, Troy. Three, two . . ." James dug his fingers into Troy's cut and he bucked in agony, but Asher refused to feel sympathy for the man in front of him.

"That was only a millimeter. An inch an hour," James said in a singsong voice. "On the count of three. Now, take a deep breath, Troy," he said, mockingly. "Three, two—"

Asher looked up at a violently shaking Troy. His eyes rolled back in his head and his labored breaths came out like whispered screams, but he didn't utter a word.

"How are you feeling?" James asked, mockingly as he massaged the torn skin on Troy's face, ripping it farther. Blood bubbled out, sliding down Troy's throat.

James's phone rang and he paused to take the call. Asher watched him flip from torturer to businessman in a split second.

"Thanks," he said before ending the call. He looked at Asher, tilting his head to the door.

Asher had no idea what was going on, but he stood on legs that were a little weak beneath him.

James crouched in front of Troy. "Don't worry, I'll be back in a minute." He stood and walked out of the room and Asher followed.

"He's not going to break," James said as he closed the door behind them. "And if I keep going, the torture will kill him. I'd still like him alive at this stage."

Asher's eyebrows threaded together. "How do you know he's not going to break?"

James sighed. "Because there's only two types of people that don't break: the ones who are insane, and the ones who are devout. Troy is the latter, and he believes so deeply in his convictions that he's prepared to die for the cause. I've run into his kind before."

"The cause to ruin my family because we're so inept that we would destroy Santina?" Asher asked, bitterly.

James nodded sympathetically. "They're his convictions, but that doesn't mean they're well founded."

"Yet he's managed to assemble a group of people who clearly think the same. How many Santinians believe it too?" he asked, not actually expecting James to have an answer. Asher pinched the bridge of his nose. "What's the plan now?"

"Samuel was able to see Troy entering the station on CCTV footage. The team is working on tracking him back through the streets to see where he came from. We have twenty-four hours to find Alistair's son—that part is likely true—so we need to use every minute of that time. Troy isn't going to give us anything so I'm not going to waste my time. I'll work with Samuel and see what we can find. We're also running some logistics on his cell phone. It's an untraceable device but we might be able to get something from it."

Asher sighed heavily. "Okay," he said, unable to ignore the churning deep in his stomach.

How many Santinians believed he was going to fail?

Maybe they were right.

James's eyes looked behind Asher. He turned to see Reed approaching.

"There's nothing more you can do right now," James said. "I'll keep you updated."

Asher sighed heavily. "I'll go to my office."

"I'll walk with you," Reed said and Asher noted the stitches on his cheek.

"Yeah, I'm not impressed," Reed said, following his gaze.

Asher didn't miss the smirk on James's face. "Your face looks a lot better than his did after you bludgeoned it."

Reed looked through the viewing window. "Now you've made a mess of my masterpiece," he said dryly.

Asher looked to James. "How many people have you skinned alive?" he asked. He didn't really want to know the answer, but he thought he should probably know.

The man paused, as if seeming to have to mentally count them all.

Asher shook his head. "I don't need the details," he said, holding up a hand.

James paused, then nodded. "I should've given you warning but my plan changed once he started talking," he said with sympathy, a stark contrast from the man who had been holding the scalpel a few minutes ago. "I will do whatever is needed to protect you, Asher. And to do that, I need to be efficient. I could've pulled his fingernails or sliced off his ear, but that all takes time—time we possibly don't have."

Asher nodded once. He understood the logic, but he wasn't sure what disturbed him most—what he'd just seen, or that he hadn't made a move to stop it.

Asher wasn't sure he was going to recognize the man he saw in the mirror tonight.

ABI

Abi heard the water running when she walked into the living quarters. She made a cup of tea and settled on the couch before turning on the television, not caring what she watched.

When the program ended some time later, she realized almost an hour had passed—and the shower was still on.

She put her tea on the table and ran for the bathroom, then opened the door, not even bothering to knock.

Abi expected to find him on the floor, but instead Asher was there standing tall, his head tilted back, letting the water fall on his face.

The sight stopped her, and for a moment she couldn't look away.

She cleared her throat. "Asher?"

He opened his eyes. There was something off about him, but she couldn't put her finger on it. She thought he might be uncomfortable or embarrassed standing naked in the shower. It wasn't like she hadn't seen him naked before, but still . . .

Instead he curled two fingers and motioned her in.

She raised her eyebrow and then decided she couldn't think of a good reason not to join him.

She slid her pants over her hips, letting them fall to the floor then lifted her top over her head and threw it with her pants. Asher undressed her with his eyes as she threw her lingerie on the pile. He held out his hands and welcomed her in.

"Hey," he said as she wrapped her arms around him.

"Hey. Are you okay?" she asked gently. "You've been in here a long time."

"I felt... I don't know," he said, shaking his head.

Abi looked at him, biting her lip. "Why?" she asked.

He gave a crooked smile. "I'm scared of James Thomas. Hell, I'm scared of myself."

Abi looked up at him, almost laughing at the odd expression on his face—except there was nothing funny about it. It was like he couldn't decide if he was sad or darkly amused.

"What happened?" she asked.

Asher paused for a moment, then shuddered. "Apparently James thought I needed a lesson in removing a man's face." He looked away from her. "The most disturbing thing is that I watched him and didn't make a move to stop it. I don't even think I flinched."

"Hmm," she muttered, not entirely sure what to say.

"It's an efficient and effective torture technique," Asher said, like it was a phrase he was repeating. "Supposedly, anyway, but Troy's not talking."

Abi's eyebrows lifted. "He didn't break?" She couldn't believe that—Abi didn't think she'd be able to hold out if James Thomas was cutting her face off.

Asher's jaw set and his eyes darkened. "This all started because they thought my father was useless and that I would be too. They killed Noah because he found out about their plan." He shook his head sharply. "Everything my father did was for this kingdom. He served Santina well. I don't care if they doubt me, but to disregard everything my father contributed? To the point where they were willing to kill him to end his reign? I can't..." he said, his voice strangling.

Abi cupped his cheek. "That is not what Santina thinks. The opinion of Troy and his little minority is not the opinion of the majority of your people. Look at their support for you, Asher. They believe in you."

"Maybe they're right about me. Maybe I'm not fit to lead," Asher said, closing his eyes and tipping his head back.

"Maybe that's what they want you to believe," Abi said slowly. "Troy's still playing games with you. Even now."

Asher opened his eyes and looked at her.

"Don't give him that power. Use your anger to prove him—and all of those who think the same way—wrong. Use it as motivation," she urged.

"I don't even know who I am right now," Asher whispered, as if he was scared to admit it. "What I just saw should've made my skin crawl, but I justified it in my mind and I sat there and watched it," he said absently, seeming to go back to that moment.

"You won't be the same person tomorrow that you were yesterday, Asher, and you certainly won't be the same person next year. You'll do whatever it takes to save Santina, and that's something you should be proud of," Abi told him, meaning every word.

Asher's eyes locked on hers and she brushed her lips over his. He gave a deep moan and turned her around, backing her up against the shower wall. She knew he was using sex as a distraction, but she didn't care. If that helped him cope, so be it.

"I really like this idea," he said, planting kisses up the soft skin of her neck.

She felt him harden against her waist.

He moaned into her ear. "You feel so good," he whispered.

His hands slid down to her ass. He leaned into her, pressing her back flat against the wall. He licked the droplets of water running over her collarbone, up to the soft space below her ear. Abi closed her eyes as he sucked on her earlobe, and heat exploded deep in her belly. A soft moan fell from her lips and she barely recognized the sound of her voice. Asher groaned in response.

One hand trailed up her inner thigh, causing her to shudder. She rocked her hips forward into his hands. Her body screamed for more.

His fingers slid through her wet folds and brushed over her clit. He teased the small bud mercilessly. Her body wound tight, coiled and waiting for more.

Abi's entire body shook, and it only seemed to encourage Asher.

"I need you, please," she begged. She was not above begging, especially not now.

"I'll give you everything you need," he said in a throaty voice, and Abi didn't think he was just talking about sex.

Her breathing was rapid and she wrapped her arms around his neck, pulling him in. Only a few inches separated them, but that was still too much.

"Asher," she moaned as the heat deep in her hips built. Her entire body ached for him.

"I love it when you say my name like that," he said huskily as he pushed two fingers inside her, and her world exploded. She folded into him, letting him hold her as her legs gave way beneath her. She rocked against him, grinding as she reeled from her orgasm. Asher gave her a minute, his hands soothing her, bringing her back to earth.

He lifted her chin, guiding her eyes to him. Their gaze locked, and she felt the tip of his hard cock before it pushed into her, stretching her wide. His eyes stayed on hers, never looking away, as he continued to rock in and out of her. He'd captured her eyes and her soul, and she was lost. In that moment, she never wanted to be found. There was something about the look in his eyes, and the domination with which he demanded her gaze—it was the most erotic thing she'd ever seen. She'd hardly been a virgin before Asher, but she'd never had a lover like him.

But then, when did Asher ever follow the rules? He made his own rules, and his train was one she didn't want to get off of. She was along for the ride—in and out of the bedroom.

He released a low, guttural moan that sounded more like a groan. Abi's breath hitched in response, and that only seemed to encourage him further. He pressed his palms into the wall and pushed harder, slamming into her, unleashing everything he'd been holding in.

Then he broke the hold on her gaze and his mouth came crashing down, consuming her as his body shuddered and he slowed.

Abi kissed his shoulder, letting her lips linger.

"Fuck me," Asher swore as he nuzzled into the crook between her neck and shoulder. He nipped and sucked the delicate skin softly and Abi opened her neck to him.

Slowly, his breathing settled and he pushed against the wall once more. He stood straight, peering into her eyes. He wore an arrogant smirk, seemingly pleased with his performance.

Abi grinned. "Yes, you just blew my mind," she said, her own throat husky.

Asher chuckled. "I don't know where that just came from."

She cupped his face. "Well, I want more of that," she said, earning herself another chuckle.

He sighed and then straightened. "How long have I been in here?"

Abi raised an eyebrow at his sudden shift. "I don't know. I could hear the water running when I came into the apartment. I waited about an hour before I came in. I was worried . . ."

He paused, kissing her forehead. "I need to get dressed. They might have an update on Alistair's son. I only meant to have a quick shower . . . but I got lost in my thoughts." He shook his head, then pulled back, using the running water to clean himself and then her.

He turned off the shower and reached around the glass, grabbing two towels. He dried himself quickly and then threw the towel over Abi's head and began drying her hair like her mother had done for her when she was a child. The unexpected tenderness made her giggle.

He pushed the towel back and it fell around her shoulders. He reeled her in, taking a moment to kiss her softly. There was no heat nor neediness in this kiss. Nothing but love.

"Come sit in the office with me," he said—more of a command than a question, but Abi was happy to oblige.

She nodded and followed him out of the shower.

She found a fresh set of clothes and when she turned around to pull her hair up into a bun she was surprised to see Asher in jeans and a T-shirt. He was almost always dressed in a suit, but she had to admit, she liked that T-shirt. It exposed his sculpted arms and she fought the urge to drag him back into the shower.

He turned away, fastened his watch around his wrist and pulled on a pair of runners. This was definitely an Asher she wasn't accustomed to seeing, but one she really liked. And she felt lucky—privileged even—to be the one who saw the king in a light few others did.

She shook her head, snapping back into gear. She pinned a loose strand of hair up, put on a thin coat of lip gloss and grabbed a sweater from the closet.

Asher held out his hand and, threading his fingers between hers, led them out of the bedroom, security encircling them as they walked to his office.

ASHER

Asher entered his office and his eyes landed on a count-down graphic in the corner of the screen. He blew out a long breath.

Samuel looked up from his computer for the briefest of moments, peering into the screen. He mumbled a hello and returned his attention to his computer, typing impossibly fast. Asher noted the large cup of coffee beside his computer and wondered how many shots of espresso were in it.

Deacon appeared on the screen. "Hi, Asher."

"Hey," Asher said, taking a seat at his desk. "Where are we?"

"We were hoping we would get lucky backtracking Troy's movements from the station." He gave a small shake of his head. "But we can't see him, which likely means he was dropped off in the underground parking garage and used the emergency stairwell to enter. Given that Troy told us we have less than twenty-four hours, we need to look at everyone involved in this, but of significant importance is the mother of the child—Isabella. Her phone wasn't on her when Reed found her, and I've been trying to trace it since but I wasn't able to find it . . . until an hour ago."

Samuel sounded excited but he didn't look up.

"Isabella's phone is a traceable device, indicating that either she wasn't involved in the revolt, or she had two phones."

Deacon looked to him. Samuel held up one finger and then nodded. "Got it," he said with a wide smile.

"Her phone is at a supermarket three blocks from here," Samuel said, then pressed his earlobe. "James, I'm sending you the address now. I'm trying to access the market's security system to see who's carrying it and estimate how long they'll still be there."

Samuel nodded, but Asher couldn't hear James's response.

"Copy," Deacon said and then looked to Asher. "James and Reed are in the garage with teams ready to go. They're leaving now."

"Okay," Asher said, his eyes dropping to the countdown clock again. He couldn't decide if seeing it was unsettling, or if it was good to know how much time they had. It was one less unknown in the sea of unknowns that surrounded them.

Abi took his hand and gave it a gentle squeeze.

"Does Alistair know?" she asked in a hushed whisper.

"No, I haven't told him. I thought it best to wait and see . . ." His voice trailed off. He couldn't bring himself to say what he was thinking: he didn't want to tell Alistair until they found the boy alive and well and were able to bring him home.

Abi nodded, understanding. She gave his hand another squeeze.

Asher's attention snapped back to the screen. He could no longer see Samuel but he could see inside a supermarket. Asher searched the aisles for any familiar faces, and his jaw fell open when he found himself looking at the woman he'd seen in the photos on Noah's computer.

The same woman they'd found dead the night they took captive Captain Lewis Spencer.

The angles adjusted—at Samuel's doing, Asher assumed. He must've seen her before Asher, because the footage changed and suddenly Asher was looking directly at her. She lifted her gaze as if she could feel them watching her, and Asher froze, suddenly feeling like she was watching him.

"Yes!" Samuel said as he began typing furiously.

Deacon looked to Asher. "Samuel was moving the camera, hoping it would create some sound—some cameras make a whirling kind of noise—and she would look straight up at the camera."

"Reed, she's holding a small basket. You might only have a few minutes," Samuel said.

Asher leaned forward, massaging his aching jaw. He made a conscious effort to relax it. How was this happening?

His eyes dropped to the clock again. The minutes seemed to be passing like seconds.

Samuel didn't look up from his computer, and Asher didn't want to bother him.

They sat in silence but the tension was palpable. This was the ultimate deadline and with every second that passed, Asher's chest grew a little tighter.

"She's leaving!" Samuel said suddenly.

Deacon leaned forward like he was looking at something. His eyes narrowed, confirming Asher's suspicions. "It's not her," he said to Asher, then added, "they look very similar, but the features don't match on facial recognition. For a second I wondered if she had a twin."

Asher's mind was spinning. A woman who looked so much like Isabella, and who had her phone?

"Talk to her, Reed," Deacon commanded.

Deacon turned to Asher. "This is interesting—it could be a good lead."

The woman exited the store, meeting Reed in the doorway. Reed didn't look like a local but Asher wasn't sure that's what gave him away. The woman took one look at him and tried to run but Reed reached out, subduing her and dragging her out of view. Asher wondered what that looked like on the street, or if any civilians were going to try and stop him, but no one said anything indicating as much.

Deacon returned his attention to Asher. "They'll drive somewhere secure and talk to her. Give them a few minutes."

How many minutes did they have?

Asher nodded and looked over his desk, needing something to distract himself for a few minutes. He picked up a folder of reports then put it down as quickly. His heel bounced on the floor. No matter how hard he tried, he couldn't tear his eyes away from the timer.

"What is your name?" Reed's voice sounded through his office.

"Lisa," she said quickly. *"Lisa!"*

"Lisa who?" Reed asked.

"Lisa Ramsey," she said, her voice a notch higher.

"Why do you have Isabella George's phone?" Reed asked.

"What?" she asked, sounding genuinely confused.

"This phone. Where did you get it?"

"It's my boyfriend's. He has two phones—one is for work—and I accidentally dropped my phone when I left the house this morning. I grabbed this phone from the charger quickly in case I needed to call anyone."

"Who is your boyfriend?" Reed asked.

"Jason King," she said.

"Was the phone off?"

A moment passed. *"Yes,"* she said, nodding. *"Why? And who is Isabella George?"* she asked, sounding less than pleased.

"A woman who was murdered a few nights ago," Reed said, seemingly to test her. Lisa's face blanched.

"What?" she asked with a hoarse voice.

"We're still looking for her murderer and, as part of the investigation, we've been looking for her phone—until now," Reed said. *"When did you see your boyfriend last?*

"This morning," she said quickly. *"His house."*

"What is his address?"

She paused. *"I don't know you."*

Reed pulled out a badge. *"Santina police,"* he said and Asher wondered when and how he'd gotten that badge.

She sighed, seeming to weigh her options, but then she gave them the address for an apartment downtown.

"Lisa, do you have a family member you can stay with for a few days?"

She looked hesitant.

*"Stay with them. Don't go back to your apartment for a while. In addition

to your boyfriend having a dead woman's phone, there's something else you should be aware of: she looks exactly like you."

Her jaw fell open and she sat back. *"What?"*

Reed nodded. *"You need to be very careful right now. Stay with family and I'll be in contact and let you know when it's safe to go home."*

"I want to go," she said quickly, looking as though she might vomit.

Reed nodded again and opened the door, letting her walk away.

Asher looked between Samuel and Deacon, trying to read their thoughts. He didn't know what to make of that conversation.

"Let's see who you are, *Jason King*," Samuel said with a quiet determination.

"This is good," Deacon said, looking at Asher. "Having an alias is a good starting point. We can find out who he is, look at CCTV and apartment security and see if we can get a match. And then we'll track assets, including property. It's a good lead," he said again.

It might be a good starting point, but Asher felt like they were losing the race.

"Why don't you get some rest?" Deacon asked. "This might take a few hours."

Asher looked to the timer. They had less than eight hours.

* * *

ASHER CHECKED his phone for the millionth time but there was no update, no contact from the team. What were they doing?

He willed his eyes to close, but they remained open. He stared at the ceiling as Abi's breath settled beside him, then his eyes darted to the neon green numbers of his bedside clock.

Four hours.

Asher sighed as he sat up. He couldn't sleep and it was harder not knowing what was going on.

"Asher?" Abi asked groggily.

"Yeah, I'm going to go back to my office. I can't sleep," he said.

She sat upright. "I'll come with you," she said.

He was going to tell her to stay there and get some rest, but he preferred her company and it could be a long night.

She picked up her clothes from the floor, put them on, and slipped on her shoes.

They'd taken a step outside the bedroom when Samuel called.

"Asher, Jason King was an alias for Troy. We've found a property Jason King bought a few months ago which Troy happened to visit yesterday. Reed's going in now."

REED

Reed crept along the fence of the neighboring property. He stopped at the sight of footprints and paused. They were pointed at the fence and then disappeared. Whoever they belonged to had recently scaled this fence. Why?

He peered over the fence quickly at the fresh footprints on the other side.

Reed looked at the print again. It was smaller than his, but he couldn't tell if it belonged to a male or female. He took a picture for Samuel—he might be able to match it to a particular brand of shoes if it was later deemed important.

He couldn't be sure if it was important to this mission or not, but it was certainly odd, and Reed had learned to pay close attention to anything that didn't seem right.

"Prints continue from the fence. I can't see for sure, but it looks like they lead to the back-left window of the house," he said quietly.

The alarm system of the neighbor's house, whose backyard Reed was currently in, was activated, telling them no one was home, so Reed didn't have to worry about being seen in the yard—by the home owners, at least.

His eyes dropped to the footprints again. Whoever made them

hadn't retreated from the window, which meant they'd either been captured and carried inside or they'd gone through the window.

Reed pulled a pair of binoculars from his kit and looked at the window in question, then swore under his breath—the window had been jammed.

"Someone paid a visit before we got here," Reed whispered.

"Then we need to move fast," James responded. *"Confirm positions."*

"Team A in position. Team B in position . . ." The confirmations kept coming. They had six teams on site because they knew the consequences of their failure would be fatal. The pressure of such a mission could asphyxiate someone not trained to handle it; any case involving children was always more difficult.

"Moving in," Reed said as he lowered into a crouch. He was the only one not technically part of a team on this mission. Reed was at his best when he moved on his own. He'd always been like that—a bit of a loner. His childhood had set him up for it, and now he used it to his advantage.

Reed sprinted for the window, following the footprints. He focused on his breathing and kept his heart rate steady as he moved, and stilled the instant he reached the wall.

He pressed his back against it, straining to listen.

There were no sounds other than a passing car at the front of the property. He paused, waiting for the team to tell him if that car was going to be a problem—but when no one spoke, he returned his attention to the jammed window.

Definitely a break-in. And a bad one.

"Amateur break-in," Reed said. Using the amateur's work to his advantage, he carefully slid his scalpel in and along the bottom of the frame until he felt the clasp. He jimmied the window and pried it open with his fingers.

He paused again, but the only sound he could hear was his own heart drumming in his chest.

"Clear," Reed whispered as he pulled two robots from his kit and dropped them on the other side of the window.

"Give me a few minutes," Samuel said quickly.

Reed looked up, his eyes scanning the eaves for surveillance cameras.

"Every door in the hallway is shut," Samuel said. "*I can't get underneath them. You'll have to go in.*"

This was becoming a problem for Samuel's robots—a problem they hadn't anticipated. They needed to design a smaller robot—one that could get underneath Santina's doors.

"Copy," Reed said as he inched the window wider. He could use the door, but he wasn't sure if it would activate an alarm. If the window had triggered an alarm, they would know by now.

"Going in," Reed said as he placed his gloved hands on the window sill, leaned forward and pushed up, holding his weight while he slid one leg over and then the other. He rushed toward the wall behind the door and took a second to assess the house.

White walls, a white sofa, and wooden floorboards. Everything was in place and looked like it should belong in such a house.

Reed darted across the doorway, getting a view of the hallway.

No motion. No sound.

The house was deadly quiet.

"House appears empty," Reed said in a hushed whisper.

"*Keep moving. Let's find out,*" James said. "*Team A, follow Reed in.*"

Reed stepped into the hallway. The floorboards creaked with every step he took. If someone was inside and they were relatively alert, they should realize someone was in the house. He stayed close to the wall, where the boards were less likely to creak.

Pausing at the first door, he waited, listening. He held his breath, not wanting to miss the sound of the slightest movement. He took an extra second and then opened the door.

The room was completely empty, but the impressions on the carpet told Reed that furniture had been there before being recently removed.

"Someone has been clearing out this apartment," Reed said under his breath.

"*If he's gone, let's find a clue they left behind. We need something to work from,*" James said.

"Copy," Reed said. He went to move forward, but his foot paused mid-air as he caught the glisten of the wire. Reed sucked in a breath, grabbing the doorframe to stop himself from hitting it.

He breathed hard, his eyes following the wire.

"James, the house is rigged," Reed said, a rushed whisper. "The footprints leading to the window, it's a setup. The first room wasn't rigged, a ploy to give us false security. Get everyone out!"

"Team A, exit the same way you came in!" James commanded.

Reed looked up to the ceiling and down to the floorboards. If he took one wrong step, it would be the last one he ever took.

The fact that someone had taken the time to rig the house meant one of only two things. Either Troy had set this up from the beginning in the event he'd be killed or captured as his final fuck-you to Asher—or there was simply something valuable inside that he didn't want anyone to find.

Reed prayed it was the latter.

He pulled a scanning device from his kit and moved to the next room. It started beeping as soon as he pressed the device against the door.

Reed looked over his shoulder at the empty hallway. The only comfort in being in a rigged house was that he didn't think it was swarming with men, unless those men had a suicide wish. Even if they knew where the trips were, if things got out of control, it would be so easy to accidentally trigger an explosion.

"There's something on the other side of this door. I can't open it," Reed said quietly. He quickly counted the doors in the hallway. Six doors remained. He moved to the next one, his heart thumping in his chest with every step he took. He kept the scanning device in his hands, but that was no guarantee. A tripping mechanism could be anything—and substances like fishing wire were hard to detect. Reed's device would detect the bomb it was linked to, but it might be too late.

He paused at the next door and scanned it. Nothing.

Here goes, he thought as he put his hand on the door knob, turning it. He didn't dare breathe.

The door opened to reveal another empty room. His eyes swept from left to right, floor to ceiling. Nothing.

Next door.

One foot in front of the other, Reed crept along the hallway. He focused on his breathing, refusing to allow his mind to run away with worst-case scenarios.

He scanned the door, and when he didn't receive an alert he slowly pushed it open. Reed wondered why the first door he'd approached had been a sliding door, and from what he could see from his position, the rest seemed to swing open. Had it been pure luck that he'd approached the door first? If he'd gone to the room next to it, he almost certainly would've been killed the second he opened the door.

He shook his head as if to shake the fatal scenarios from his mind. Right now, he needed only to think about what was in front of him.

He pushed the door open, revealing another empty room—but this time he noted more unusual impressions on the carpet.

"James, he was here. There was a small bed or crib in this room. I'm almost certain of it," he said, angling his chest so that Samuel would be able to see the impressions via his camera.

"Agreed," James said.

Reed went to move to the next room when he smelled it: the unmistakable woody scent of something burning.

"*Reed, I have a heat sensor coming from the back of the house,*" Samuel said quickly.

"Confirm, I can smell it," he said. He needed to move fast, he knew, but the rigging of the house made that impossible.

Reed eyed the front door, moving carefully toward it, then ran the scanner. When he didn't receive an alert, he slid the bolt and opened the door. He paused, waiting for a reaction, but the house didn't go up in flames.

He looked back to the hallway. He couldn't see the smoke yet, so he had some time, and he had an exit through the front door.

He ran back to the door he'd been ready to open, careful to trace his steps.

Reed wedged the door open and his eyes widened in response.

Perhaps he'd been wrong about the impressions belonging to a crib, because this room was a nursery. It was all white. White walls, white carpet, white furniture—it was eerily white. He scanned for a trip wire but couldn't see anything, and so he took one cautious step forward and then another.

He paused, his breath catching in his throat as he saw the bedding in the crib. It was soaked red.

"James . . ." Reed started.

"I see it. It looks like real blood, but I doubt it's the child's. They need him for leverage. Keep looking," James said.

"Copy," Reed said.

His eyes caught the fireplace as he turned to leave, but something made him turn back around.

"Reed, that fire is growing wild. You have a few minutes at most," Samuel said, but Reed had already gathered as much based on the smoke filling his lungs.

Reed inched toward the fireplace, every sense alert and ready.

He stood in front of it and ran a finger along the join that had caught his attention. It was slightly cracked, pulling apart at the join. Reed knew from his carpentry days—how he'd spent every weekend working while he was at school—that stone didn't crack like that.

He ran his finger over it and knew straight away it wasn't real stone, but rather a laminate of some kind.

And Reed knew why.

Reed ran his fingers along the edge, feeling for a latch or button. Nothing.

He ran his fingers along the top. Nothing.

He crouched low, peering into the wooden logs. He placed a hand on one and pulled it forward. He heard the click and then the entire fireplace moved, revealing a door below.

"Reed, you need to get out!" Samuel's voice came through, urgent and less controlled than usual.

"One minute," Reed responded as he heard the soft wailing of a child. He couldn't give up now.

Reed coughed and lifted his T-shirt, covering his mouth and nose as he stepped forward. He stood at the top of the stairs, knowing if he went down, they could be rigged. There was also every chance the fire would spread and he'd be trapped.

But he could hear a child crying.

Reed's eyes scanned for wires, cameras, or anything that might set off a trap.

He moved fast as he could while still being cautious of his surroundings. He couldn't help the boy if he was dead.

"Reed," James said, a warning.

"I can hear him," Reed said.

A moment passed before James answered. *"You might not get back out."*

Reed already knew that. He took a step forward and then another. He pulled a flashlight from his kit, choosing to keep the lights off—it was easier to see fishing wire in the glow of a flashlight than in a well-lit room. The sound of the baby's cries intensified as he reached the bottom, and then he saw a crib in the corner of the basement.

He stilled when he noticed the body next to it: a woman sat in the chair with a bullet between her eyes, execution style.

Reed spun around, sweeping his torch over the basement, but he didn't hear or see anything. He darted for the light switch, held his breath as he turned it on and exhaled when the basement didn't blow up.

Smoke lingered at the top of the stairs, reminding Reed to move—now.

"Samuel, can you see her?" Reed asked.

"Copy. Confirm adequate for facial recognition. Get out!"

Reed darted to the crib, picked up the little boy and ran for the stairs, taking them two at a time.

He rushed into the room and into a wall of smoke.

He held the baby to his chest, pulling his T-shirt over his head. Reed looked to the flames licking the door frame.

His pulse raced.

He looked to the window and ran to it, but his heart sank as he looked at the wire running across it.

"I'm trapped," Reed said, his voice a whisper.

"No you're not," James's response came strong and fast. *"Don't you dare give up now. Look up, is there a trap door in the ceiling?"*

Reed's head snapped back, spotting the trap door above the window.

Reed coughed, his lungs suffocating on the acrid smoke.

"Confirm," he said, starting to choke.

"Get into the ceiling and crawl toward the front. Drop into the room closest to the front door. Move!"

Reed put the baby down on the floor as he dragged a chest of drawers underneath the trap door. He pressed his fingertips up and pushed the cover aside—then, with a hand on each side, he hauled himself up just long enough to see if he could crawl through. The roof was hazy from the smoke but it was Reed's only option.

He lowered down, coughing so hard it sounded like he was hacking up a lung. He grabbed the little boy, who was quiet now, his eyes closed.

Reed shook him gently and he stirred.

He had to get them out—and he needed two hands to do that.

Reed grabbed the bloody sheet from the crib and tore it. It was hardly ideal to use as a makeshift baby carrier, but it was all he had.

"Sorry, kid," Reed whispered as he wrapped the bloody linen around the baby, securing him to his chest just as a lump of something fell to the floor. Reed didn't take another look at it; he didn't want to know.

With his hands free, he pulled himself into the ceiling. It took everything he had and he remained on his hands and knees, wheezing.

"Reed, move!" James commanded, breaking through the haze.

Reed crawled along the beams as smoke settled into the base of his lungs.

He was fighting for every breath, and the smoke was filling the ceiling space so quickly he was no longer sure he was even going in the correct direction.

"The trap doors likely line up. Feel with your hands. Keep moving forward," James commanded, his voice calm and controlled.

Reed stayed on the beam, moving as quickly as he could. He swayed and lost his balance, and his arm shot out instinctively, landing on something hot. He didn't know if it was fire or a light bulb, but he hissed as he pulled his burning hand back. He tried to move forward but couldn't bear any weight on the hand.

"Reed, keep going, you're almost there. Keep going," James said.

Reed turned his hand over, crawling on one palm and on the top of his injured hand. He coughed again, his vision blurring.

Keep going.

He crawled forward, but he had no idea how far he was actually moving. He didn't know if he was moving at all. He felt stuck, like the smoke had placed him in an invisible trap.

"*Keep going. One hand in front of the other. Keep moving,*" James urged, sounding out of breath.

Reed wheezed and the beam below him shifted.

"*Keep...*"

He wheezed as he felt the darkness pull him under.

ASHER

He sat in his office, holding his own breath. He didn't look at Abi; his eyes were glued to the screen.

"I'm going in for him," James said, sounding like he was running. The screen changed and Asher leaned forward, watching the footage stream from James's camera. Judging by the view, Asher assumed it was fastened to his shirt, but he couldn't be sure.

A second footage stream activated in the corner of the screen. Asher narrowed his eyes but he couldn't see anything. It was like looking out of an airplane window as it flew through the clouds.

He pinched the back of his neck.

It didn't look like Reed was moving at all, and that likely meant the baby was unconscious too.

"Hurry," Asher whispered under his breath, and Abi put a comforting hand on his thigh.

James entered through the front door into a wall of smoke. Asher couldn't see flames, and he didn't know if that was a good thing or not. Were there none in the hallway? Or was the smoke so thick the flames were veiled?

James opened a hallway door and cautiously stepped inside.

Asher heard a beeping noise and his stomach churned.

"The trap door is rigged," James said quickly, and it was the closest to panicked that Asher had ever heard him.

James darted across the hallway and into the room opposite.

When he swore, Asher felt like James was kicking him in the stomach. They were so close, but the mission now seemed impossible.

"Jackson, get in here!" James commanded. *"First door on the right."*

"Copy," said an unfamiliar voice.

"Jackson is a bomb expert," Samuel said through the speaker system, answering Asher's unspoken question, and he wondered once again if Samuel had some kind of device that could read his mind.

Yet another footage stream flashed up on the screen. Asher's jaw clenched and he fought the bile rising in his chest. How long had Reed and the boy been unconscious? Even if James reached them, would they be okay?

"Samuel, we're going to need full medics on site," James said, mirroring Asher's concerns.

"Already on their way," Samuel responded calmly.

"Copy," James said.

James and Jackson discussed the rigging of the trap door. Asher didn't understand a word of what they were saying, but he knew how to read someone's tone of voice—they were worried.

"There's nothing I can do from this side. I need to get into the ceiling space, but if I open that trap door there's a chance this whole house will blow," Jackson said quickly.

"What do you think the chances of that are?" James asked.

A pause followed. "I don't know. Maybe fifty-fifty. Less if we're lucky."

"Samuel, how are Reed's vitals?" James asked.

"Not good, and neither are yours. You need to get him out, or you need to leave," Samuel said as James sounded like he was suppressing a cough.

Abi sucked in a breath beside him but Asher couldn't tear his eyes away from the screen.

"Go!" James commanded.

"No, I can help," Jackson insisted.

"Go!" James commanded again.

Asher saw Jackson walk through the front door.

"*Samuel, if—*" James started.

"No," Samuel said, cutting him off. "Get in and get out. Come on."

A painfully long moment passed, and then the camera angled up to the ceiling, indicating James had made his decision.

"*Give her the envelope,*" James said as he reached his arms up.

"Not yet," Samuel said.

What envelope?

Give it to who?

Asher had so many questions, but he knew now was not the time. Right now he needed to stay quiet and let them do their thing.

James pressed his fingertips to the trap door, muttered something under his breath and then lifted it. He paused, seeming to brace for impact, but it didn't come.

James moved so fast if Asher had blinked he would've missed it. And then he was presumably crawling—though given the speed he was moving at, that seemed impossible to Asher.

Visibility through the smoke was nonexistent.

"Two more meters, you're heading straight toward him," Samuel said, sounding excited.

James coughed and Asher couldn't tell if he was moving or not. But a moment later, he said, *"I have him!"*

Asher almost stood up and cheered. He looked to Abi, who wore a big smile. Her eyes were straight ahead, watching the footage.

But, the reality of the situation suffocated his excitement. James still had to get them out of the ceiling space. And by the time he did that, would it be too late?

"Come on," Asher thought he heard Samuel whisper.

"James, you need to move faster," Samuel said then, loud and clear.

"*I'm trying,*" James responded with an odd tone to his voice. Asher couldn't decide if he was irritated, amused, or losing consciousness.

"Almost there! Almost there! Faster!" Samuel said.

When they were through, he heard Samuel breathe a sigh of relief.

"Medics have arrived, James. Jackson and his team are coming up, they'll help lift them down," Samuel said, the calm controller back.

"*Copy,*" James said, his voice a wheeze.

Asher folded his arms across his chest and leaned back, forcing himself to relax. He was going to get a tension migraine if he continued to watch Thomas Security's missions. He'd witnessed more than enough excitement for a lifetime.

Multiple footage streams activated on the screen and Asher's eyes darted from one to the next, watching as James's men lowered the boy out first, Reed, and then James—who appeared barely conscious.

Medics rushed in, put them on stretchers, and wheeled them away. The screen went blank.

"Asher, they'll be taken to the hospital. James will recover quickly, but Reed and the boy may be there for some time—a few days at least."

"Thank you," Asher said, standing.

"You're welcome," Samuel said. "I'll keep you updated, but so far the information coming from the ambulance is that the patients are stable. That's the best we can hope for at this stage."

"Thank you," Asher said again as Abi stood too.

He grabbed her hand and led her out of the office.

"Where are we going?" she asked.

"To find Alistair," he responded, heading toward his brother's living quarters.

As they approached the kitchen, Abi pulled her hand away.

"You go and deal with this with Alistair. I'll wait here," she said, understandingly.

Asher kissed her forehead. "I'll be back as soon as I can," he said before letting her go.

Abi nodded and gave him a smile.

Asher strode toward Alistair's rooms. Security stood outside, indicating he was inside. He couldn't remember the last time he'd been in his brother's living quarters. It was realizations like this that made him realize how far apart they'd grown without even noticing.

A memory flooded Asher's mind, and he realized he could remember the last time he'd visited his brother. Alistair had been on a bender and, their father having just heard the news, Asher had been sent to tell his brother he was expected at dinner.

A chill swept over Asher's spine as he remember the way he'd felt when he'd walked away. But Alistair's involvement had been explained now; his brother wasn't a malicious threat.

Still, Asher felt wary knocking on his door.

The security guard at the door relayed his arrival and the door opened. Another security guard welcomed him in and escorted him to the living room.

Asher came to a halt when he saw his mother sitting with Alistair, her eyes red-rimmed. She quickly wiped the tears away. Alistair's face was impassive, but he sported dark circles under his glistening eyes.

"I'm sorry, am I interrupting?" Asher asked, suddenly feeling uncomfortable.

"No, not at all," Emilia said.

"What's up?" Alistair asked, his throat husky, indicating he was more emotional than his face portrayed.

Asher watched his brother carefully. "They found him—your son. He's stable, but there was a fire and they're taking him to the hospital to treat him for smoke inhalation—"

Alistair was out of his seat and grabbing his wallet and phone before Asher could finish.

"Why didn't you tell me you knew where he was?" Alistair asked with a hint of accusation in his voice.

"Because I didn't know if they would find him alive, or if they could rescue him," Asher admitted. He didn't think he'd have been able to watch the footage if it had been his own son.

Alistair stilled, seeming to let that sink in. "Can I see him?" he asked.

"I think we should all go," Asher said, looking past his brother to his mother.

Emilia stood and rushed to Asher. "Thank you," she whispered as she wrapped her arms around Asher. "You're a great king, and an even better brother," she said, so quietly Asher wasn't sure he'd heard her correctly.

She kissed his cheek and then hurried them to the door. Security teams had been assembled, indicating that someone—likely Samuel—had been eavesdropping on their conversation.

The men led them to the garage and escorted them in individual cars. Asher knew the reason for this, but he tried to block it from his mind.

He watched the mirrors and everything the security team did as they drove. When they arrived at the hospital without incident, Asher said a silent prayer of thanks.

They were escorted to the Pediatric Intensive Care Unit and were greeted by a nurse, who showed them into a private room.

Asher's heart stilled as he looked at the little boy sleeping in the bassinet. A mask was fitted on his face and leads hung off him everywhere, but he was alive.

Alistair exhaled a shaky breath beside him.

Asher realized he didn't even know how old the boy was. Did his brother?

He didn't think now was the right time to ask, so he stored that question for later. Samuel probably knew, he thought absently.

"Look at him," Emilia said from beside him. "He looks like you," she said with a small smile, looking to Alistair.

"Does he?" Alistair asked. He leaned over the bassinet and held the boy's hand. "Keep fighting, little prince," he whispered.

Asher glanced at his mother, who had tears streaming down her cheeks.

Emilia stepped forward, stroking the boy's cheeks. "I can't believe it," she said with a beaming smile while tears fell from her eyes. "He's perfect."

Asher looked between his brother and his mother and decided to give them a moment. There was something important he needed to do.

He checked in with security, not surprised they already had the information he needed. "Please take me to them."

Asher was encircled by security, noticing his team had seemed to double in size now that they were in a public setting.

They took the elevator down a few levels and walked a maze of hallways before stopping at a door. Security knocked and then entered.

Asher's eyes landed on James Thomas and then on Reed, who was in the bed beside him with a large oxygen mask fitted over his face. He didn't open his eyes, but Asher looked to the screen and knew enough to know he was alive.

James mustered a small smile as Asher moved toward him.

"Hey," Asher said. "Thank you. I can't thank you enough."

James shook his head slowly. "This is what we do," he said with a croaky voice.

Asher shook his head knowingly. "No, you go above and beyond."

"I won't leave a man behind. That's not who I am—it's not who we are. Anyway, he's valuable alive," James joked, gesturing toward the bed before his mood turned somber. "And I definitely wouldn't leave a child."

Asher nodded. "We owe you everything. I don't know how big your bill is going to be, but I still think it will never be enough." He grinned, even though he was honestly somewhat terrified of the bill to come.

"Oh don't worry," James said with a grin of his own, "the bill will be plenty." He chuckled. "Take a seat." He tilted his head to the chair beside the hospital bed.

Asher dragged it over.

"What is the envelope you referred to before you went up through the trap door?" Asher asked.

James's eyes were distant, as if he'd gone back to that moment in time. "An envelope for my wife and daughter." There was no smile on his face. "My job comes with considerable risks, and I'm not sure how many lives I have left. I've definitely used more than nine," he said with a lopsided grin which faded as fast as it came. "The envelope has two letters, one for Mak and one for Serena. Samuel is to give it to them when my last life is used and I don't make it home."

Asher opened his mouth to speak, but nothing seemed adequate. "I'm sorry, I didn't realize. I wouldn't have asked if I knew it was so personal."

James shrugged. "I know everything about you, Asher," he said, his grin returning. "It seems fair to share a few things about me. Anyway, the letters tell them everything I want them to remember . . . if I knew I was dying, it would be every last word I'd want to say to them. I know it won't be much of a consolation, but it'd be all I could give them."

"Why don't you retire?" Asher asked. "Why do you keep doing this?"

James looked thoughtful for a minute. "Well, I was essentially retired until we got the call from Jesse," he chuckled. "Seriously, though, it's very hard to sit back and do nothing when you receive calls from people whose lives are falling apart and they're being threatened. If you know you can help them, how can you say no?"

Asher considered that. "But at what cost? At what point do you save yourself instead of others?"

James nodded knowingly. "I know, and trust me, that is a conversation Deacon and I both had with our wives before taking your case." His eyes widened and he pulled a face. Asher grinned as he imagined that conversation. "And that's why, up until your case, Deacon and I had strategic roles only, and our bodyguards—guys like Reed—would go out in the field. But your connection to Vince made this case very different." He paused, looking at Asher. "What do you know about Vince, other than he owns a portfolio of special hotels?"

Asher tried to recall everything Jesse had told him, and he realized he knew startlingly little. "That he sets the rules and the world obeys."

James eyes swirled and a slight smile formed on his lips. "That's one way of putting it. Vince's hotels are essentially safe houses for men like me. As soon as you walk into one of his hotels, you're safe. No one will touch you. If they do, Vince will make sure they don't see sunrise. And he isn't just a man of threats; he lives by his word and he follows through regardless of who you are." James sighed. "A few years ago, his son broke the rules. Vince killed him." He shook his head. "If my daughter did that, I honestly don't know if I'd be able to follow through on the threat, but Vince did. He's one of the most respected criminals in the world, and when he gives you his word, he keeps it.

"Vince offered us a favor in return for taking this case. We don't take on new clients, we haven't for years, but Vince is a powerful man and having a favor like that up my sleeve might be the very thing that could save my family in the future. So, we made the call to take your case on. Our work has never been about money—past needing enough to live on—but it has always been about security: for our clients, and for ourselves and our families."

James looked away for a moment. "Life is a strange thing. One minute everything is smooth sailing, and the next, shit is hitting the fan and you're scared to breathe. Our lives aren't that different despite all the controls we have in place. We take every precaution we can, but we can't predict what will happen. The one thing I can control, though, is putting things in place so if all hell breaks loose, I have every contact I need. And Vince is a very handy contact should that ever happen."

Asher shook his head. "Regardless of the benefit Vince is providing, I don't think I can ever repay you."

James wore a smile but his eyes were serious. "You don't owe us anything—except the bill," he said with a quiet laugh. "And we're not done yet. Today was a huge step in the right direction. Now that you have the boy, we have Troy locked up, Abi and your mother are safe, and Lamberi is dead, you can unleash without fear. Sure, your enemies can retaliate against Santina, but the faster and harder you hit, the less likely that'll be. Your next move needs to be terrifying and unpredictable. Asphyxiate them with fear and then unleash every trick you've got up your sleeve. Strategy wins a war, and this *is* a war."

Asher's eyes blazed and a fire burned in his chest. He was ready. "And I hate to lose."

James grinned, and this time his smile reached his eyes. "Me too."

ASHER

Asher stared at the pages on his desk. He'd spent the last three hours strategizing, working out where to hit his enemies the hardest. He knew their pain points, he knew their egos, and he was ready to obliterate them. His enemies might doubt him, sometimes he doubted himself, but he would prove them wrong. He would not fail, and he would build on his father's legacy. It would be the best way to honor his father.

His eyes darted to the crystal clock and he yawned. It was midnight. He wanted to crawl into bed beside Abi, but he knew he wouldn't be able to sleep. Part of him was terrified; but surprisingly, another part of him was fired up. He wondered if this was how soldiers felt going to war.

Asher picked up the phone. "Samuel, how easily can you find information on an event that occurred eighteen months ago? I want to look at something that happened in Adani."

"I can find anything," Samuel said without hesitation, "but how easily depends on what you're looking for. What do you need?"

"I want you to look at a bacteria that contaminated some of Adani's water supply. King Khalil has been working hard to repair his reputation since then," Asher said, proceeding to give Samuel the date and event details.

"Give me twenty-four hours to work on this and I'll report back to you," Samuel said, sounding like Asher had just given him a gift.

"Thank you," Asher said before he hung up the phone.

He leaned back in his chair. *Stage one in process; now for stage two.*

Asher pulled out the sale contract for the Lithe ruins—the holy site Alistair had sold to Adani.

Testing had been completed by Thomas Security and it was indeed full of oil. As Asher read over the contract yet again, one major question glared at him, and so he picked up the phone again.

"Hello," Alistair answered.

"Hey. How is he doing?" Asher asked.

"Nurses say he's a little fighter," Alistair said, sounding proud. "God only knows what that means for my future."

Asher chuckled. "That's good to hear. Keep me updated."

"Sure," Alistair said, sounding tired. "How are the others recovering?"

Asher's eyebrows lifted. It was most unlike his brother to even think of asking after anyone else. Asher liked this version of Alistair—he hoped he was here to stay.

"James is awake and conscious. Last I heard, Reed is still unconscious but he's stable. He's receiving oxygen therapy and will hopefully awake within the next few hours."

"That's good news. I'd like to see them tomorrow," Alistair said, sounding unsure.

"I think they'd appreciate that," Asher said, hoping he sounded more confident than he felt, but he understood Alistair's need to thank them.

"Before you go . . ." Asher said, praying Alistair didn't get defensive at his next words. "I'm looking over the sale contract for Lithe. How did you know there was oil there?"

Alistair paused and Asher's stomach churned. He knew he wasn't going to like what came next.

"I received an anonymous tip," Alistair finally said.

"How did you receive this tip?" Asher asked, fighting to keep his tone neutral.

Alistair sighed. "At a party. I went to snort a line; when I came back to my seat there was an envelope with a check for one billion dollars and a phone number on the back. It wasn't a real check, obviously; I was high, but even I knew that. I phoned the number and someone gave me the details and geographical location. I had nothing better to do, so I thought I'd check it out. A few days later, I received a phone call—this one from Martin Snider. The voice was different, I was sure of it, but he offered to help me make the deal. It went from there."

"I need the date of this party, the location, and what time you think this was," Asher said, a plan formulating in his mind.

"I can give you the date and location. Time . . . Asher, I was so high I barely knew my own name, let alone what time it was," Alistair said apologetically.

"But you remembered the sound of the man's voice?"

"I phoned the next day. The envelope kind of freaked me out. I wasn't going to call, but then I did. I wish I'd never made the call. I'm sorry, Asher," he said quietly.

"I know," Asher said, and for once he actually believed his brother. "Text me the date and location and anything else you can remember."

"Give me a few minutes," Alistair said.

Asher ended the call and put his phone down on his desk. He seriously questioned what Samuel was going to be able to do with this information. He was a computer hacker, not a magician.

Asher ran his palms over his face and squeezed his eyes shut. He needed to sleep, but as he opened his eyes to stand he saw a new stack of mail he'd put aside that afternoon. He wanted to walk into an office with a clean desk tomorrow, so he quickly opened the mail and sorted it into tasks, like he'd done with Abi earlier that morning.

He paused on a package—a box small enough to fit in the palm of his hand. He knew Thomas Security scanned his mail for anything explosive, but as he held it in his hands, he couldn't shake the unease that tightened around his neck like invisible chains.

He opened the box like he was opening a box of delicate glasses. When he lifted the lid, his eyebrows rose high on his forehead.

He looked at the tape recorder, which was sitting on a white card. Slowly, he pulled out the card and glanced at the words written on its surface.

I thought you would like to know.

He flipped over the box again. No sender name, just an address. Asher would send it to Samuel, but he already thought it was a dummy address.

He turned the recorder over in his hands, his thumb resting on the play button.

Asher took a deep breath and pressed the button.

He recognized her voice immediately, but there was something different about it.

"Abigail Bennett, describe your relationship with King Asher," a male voice, one Asher didn't recognize, said.

"There is no relationship."

Asher stilled. When had this been recorded?

"You were his girlfriend, correct?"

"We dated a few times, and then . . ." Her voice trailed off.

He heard what sounded like a slap, and Abi gasped.

Asher assumed this had been recorded when she was being held. Had they drugged her?

He felt sick, but he couldn't turn the recording off.

"And then what?" the male voice demanded.

"What?" she asked, sounding confused.

Asher's eyebrows wove together.

"How long did you date the king?"

"The prince. He was a prince, not a king," she said, her words slurred.

"How long did you date the *prince*?" the man asked, sounding tired.

". . . I don't know. A few weeks, maybe," she said vaguely.

Asher knew exactly how long they'd dated. He remembered every date clearly. But then, Abi wasn't fully conscious—he could tell that from the few words she'd spoken.

"How did you meet the prince?"

Abi sighed. "Through a friend."

"Which friend?"

Abi didn't respond.

"Which friend?" the man repeated, his voice raising.

"Noah," Abi said quickly, but her voice sounded hazy, like she wasn't quite sure what she was saying—but everything she'd said so far had been true.

"Why did Noah introduce you two? Wouldn't there have been a conflict of interest?" he asked.

"There were many," she said slowly.

"But one in particular: the feud between your father and the king," the man said.

"Hmm," Abi responded, sounding like she was falling asleep again.

"Give me one good reason why Noah would introduce you two."

"IFRT," she said.

"Did Asher work for IFRT?"

"No," Abi said.

"We know he provided border permission for IFRT," a new voice said, and Asher wondered how many men were in the room with her.

"Hmm . . ." Abi mumbled.

"The prince betrayed his own father and he betrayed Santina by providing border permissions."

"Or he helped rescue hundreds of innocent women and children," Abi said, her voice sounding suddenly stronger. "Sometimes we have to tell a lie to save lives."

Asher squeezed his eyes shut.

"So you're in the habit of telling lies, Abigail Bennett?"

Asher heard the goading in his voice.

An almost maniacal laugh came from Abi. "Asks the man who kidnapped me."

"I'll take that as a yes," he said.

"Take it however you please," Abi retorted.

"What about murder?" he asked.

"What about it?" Abi responded, her voice sounding off again.

"Do you sometimes have to commit murder to save lives?"

"Sometimes," she said.

"So you're a murderer?"

"I do what needs to be done," she said flatly.

"So I've heard," he said, sounding pleased with himself. "Where were you on February second?"

A moment passed. "I have no idea," Abi said.

"Let me help you . . . IFRT rescued thirty-five women from an abandoned school," he said.

"Then that's where I would've been," Abi replied.

"And on that same day, sixteen boy soldiers were slaughtered by IFRT. Were you leading that operation?"

"Probably," she admitted.

"So you gave the order to kill the soldiers? Village boys who had been taken captive by Lamberi's men and turned into soldiers against their own will. Instead of rescuing them and returning them to their families, you slaughtered them. Isn't that right, Abigail Bennett?"

Asher couldn't breathe.

"It was self-defense, not murder. Their innocence was taken by Lamberi the day he turned them into soldiers," she said, her words running into one another.

"Did you kill them, or not?" he asked.

"Probably," she said vaguely.

Asher groaned, pressing his fingers against his temples.

"What is your plan with Asher now?"

"There is no plan," she said.

"Because you have what you want from him?"

"Because of the border permissions? He knew what I was doing, I didn't trick him," she said.

"But he didn't know who he was helping, did he? What did you tell him your name was?" the man asked.

A long pause followed.

"You lied to him, and you used him," the man said.

"I didn't lie to him," she slurred. "I just . . . failed to say the full truth."

"So there's a gray area between the truth and a lie. And that's okay, isn't it, Abigail Bennett?"

"Fuck you," Abi said sharply.

The man laughed. "A liar and a murderer. He was right—you'll never be fit to be Santina's queen."

"We'll see," Abi said defiantly, her words stronger than her voice.

Asher's eyebrows rose despite himself. What had she meant by that?

A new voice spoke next, clearer than the other voices. "That's just the start of an hour-long chat we had with your *hero* girlfriend. Do what we say—or we'll release the full recording to the media."

The tape cut off, and Asher stared at the wall. He veins pumped with fury and he fought the urge to scream until his lungs exploded. Just when he'd thought he could unleash his plan, his enemies still had leverage on him.

And he couldn't shake the questions the tape raised about Abi. She'd been drugged, she must've been, but she seemed to speak the truth. There had been something about the way she'd said it: *We'll see.*

His mind reeled with terrifying scenarios. He stood and began to pace. He spun around just as James Thomas walked in, to Asher's surprise—he wasn't even aware he'd discharged himself from the hospital.

"We're going to run some analysis on that tape and then make a plan for how to deal with it," James said.

Asher questioned whether he'd listened to the entire recording, and was certain he had.

"It's her," Asher said through gritted teeth.

"I agree," James said. "But, she was also under the influence of something—some type of sedation. Too, that recording could've been chopped and edited to make it sound worse than it is." James eyed him carefully, sitting on the edge of his desk. "What did she actually say in the recording that you didn't already know?"

Asher stared out of the window. When he didn't continue, James answered for him. "Nothing. She, and I, have already said her past isn't clean, however good her intentions."

"We understand that, but is Santina going to?" Asher asked bitterly, squeezing his eyes shut. It was yet another blow against him, and he was sick of it. He needed it all to end.

"I think this is the first recording of what will probably be a *series*. And this one just skimmed the surface of questioning Abi's past—her integrity. Why do you think they would want to do that?" James asked.

Asher knew the answer. "They couldn't take her or kill her, which would've destroyed me. So, they're doing this instead."

James nodded. "Exactly. We've dug through Abi's past—we have tracked back over the last fifteen years and found every piece of dirt on her that we could, and I've discussed it all with Jesse. If I thought for a second that she might not be who we think she is, I would've said something—that is my job as head of your security. I'm not here to make friends; I'm here to keep you alive."

"So you're not concerned about the tape?" Asher asked with raised eyebrows.

"Oh, I'm concerned," James said, "but only about how it's going to be used against you and Abi. I'm not concerned with anything she actually said. The two of you were broken up at the time and had hardly spoken, so for her to say there's nothing between you was correct. She was also sedated to some degree, but some of her words sound coherent. She might've been aware enough to know that the less she said about your relationship with her, the better. You are part of the reason she was taken—that was obvious from the first recording IFRT obtained from the hut she was being held in—so anyone in her situation with her training would know to downplay that relationship.

"Regarding the IFRT mission—she's right. If they hadn't killed the boy soldiers, the soldiers would've killed them. Murder is not black and white; it's fifty shades of gray . . . but spinning that to the public if this tape is released is not going to be so easy, I'll admit that," James said.

"Can you take it down if it's released?" Asher asked.

"It depends on how and when it's released, and how many people make copies of it. Once it's on social media, it's out of our control. Samuel can shut down a TV station network but only for so long. If your enemies want to release that tape, they will—unless you find a way to scare them so they don't dare."

Asher leaned his elbows on his knees as his head hung down. "I don't know who is behind this."

James's next words surprised him. "You don't have to know. You don't have to make your move against the person behind this tape. You just need to show them—and the world—that you're not someone to be messed with."

"And how do I do that?" Asher asked, raising his head.

"You know that case you asked Samuel to look at?" James asked, a tight smile forming on his lips.

Asher nodded.

"You won't believe what we found."

ABI

*A*bi looked at the cold, perfectly folded bed sheet beside her. Light shone through the slightly parted curtain.

Asher hadn't come to bed at all.

Abi leaned over, reaching for the remote control. She held her breath as she scrolled through the news channels, but nothing major had happened in Santina last night. She was about to call him when she heard the door open.

"Hey," he said as he walked in.

"Hi. Are you okay?" she asked.

"Sure." He walked past her to the bathroom. He closed the door behind him but she heard the running water and assumed he was brushing his teeth. He emerged a few minutes later, discarded his clothes, leaving only his boxers on, and slid in beside her. But he didn't pull her into his arms—he only closed his eyes.

"Asher," Abi said, her chest tightening when he didn't look at her.

"Hmm," he mumbled.

Had she done something wrong? If so, she couldn't think of what, and she wasn't going to play games.

"Can you look at me for a second?" she asked.

He opened his eyes, she assumed due to the tone of her voice more than anything.

"What?" he asked after a moment.

"What is going on? And don't lie to me," she said flatly, propping herself up on her elbow.

"Nothing. I've been up all night dealing with shit and I just want to sleep," he said, his tone sharp, but he was quick to realize his mistake. "I'm sorry, I'm just . . . My mind is reeling."

"Why? What happened? You said earlier that everything was my business, and now you've changed your mind."

She saw the reluctance in his eyes and turned away.

"I received a sound recording in the mail," he said, his voice wary.

"A sound recording of what?" she asked, turning back to him.

He looked away, and then back to her. Biting his lip, he said, "You. I think you were sedated."

Her jaw must've hit the floor and her body went numb. "What?" she asked, barely a whisper.

"I was going to tell you in the morning—I just wanted an hour of sleep," he said. "You sound like you're drugged—some words slur into others—but your sentences make sense. Your words are coherent," he said and her stomach churned violently. She thought of Lenna's drawing of the man with the syringe and the walls swayed.

"I want to listen to it," she told him resolutely. She didn't want to, but she needed to.

Asher sighed heavily, but she thought he was mainly just tired.

"I'm going to listen to that tape." She made a move toward the door, but Asher beat her to it.

"Give me a minute to put some pants on," he said. "I'll come with you."

She nodded as Asher headed toward the walk-in closet. Her stomach churned at the thought of the tape and what she could have said. The fear that she'd said something while sedated had been festering in the back of her mind, but now it was real.

"Where is it?" Abi asked as they entered Asher's office.

"James took the tape to run some analysis. I'll have Samuel play it for us," he said, not faltering. "Samuel!"

Abi knew they monitored everything that was said inside these walls, so surely someone would hear Asher now.

Samuel didn't respond, but James Thomas entered the room with a brief nod after only a few seconds had passed.

James looked to Abi, not wasting time. "Before I play you this recording, I want you to remember two things. You and I, and Asher to some extent, see the world very differently. We understand how things work and what it takes to get a result. There is nothing in this recording that I would judge you for, because I've done it all myself."

Abi crossed her arms over her chest, bracing herself.

She stole a look at Asher, whose eyes locked on hers. He nodded in agreement.

"Please just play the recording," Abi said. Her legs felt weak beneath her and she sat down on the chair opposite Asher's desk.

"Okay," James said, his voice calm. "Samuel, activate the recording."

The speaker on Asher's desk activated and Abi leaned forward, burying her face in her hands. A shiver ran up her spine when she heard her own voice—it sounded so foreign, but there was no mistaking it was her.

She cringed at everything she said. When she responded, *"Nothing,"* to what Asher meant to her, her head snapped to him, but he was looking at the speaker, his face unreadable.

She hadn't meant that. He had meant everything to her even then. He'd changed her world from their first date.

Abi chewed on her cheek as the recording continued and memories of the mission flashed in her mind.

But it was the ending that gave her the chills. It was something about her voice, the vindication in it. *We'll see.* She sounded manipulative and arrogant. She sounded like a player. She knew those who knew her wouldn't think that. But the people of Santina? That was a different question.

"I have no recollection of any of this," Abi said, her voice a hoarse whisper. "I was only unconscious once during captivity—I think—and

I did have concerns they'd drugged me because I remembered an IFRT case from years ago. That was the file Rachel picked up for me. Reed copied it." She shook her head, trying to organize her thoughts. "The mission, we were there, but I didn't kill any of those boy soldiers. Not that night—"

James held up his hand like he was stopping traffic, but really he was stopping the words pouring out of Abi's mouth.

"I don't want anything said about IFRT business in front of Asher. To be honest, I actually don't care if you did or not," James said unapologetically. "But we need to protect Asher from your potentially complicated past. Asher has never seen your security file, and I advised him when we took this case that I would not discuss your past with him. If I came across something I thought was a concern, I told him I would speak to Jesse and we would go from there. Although unlikely, there's a possibility that in the future Asher could be questioned about your past, and I want to make sure if he has to testify in some form or another, he can truthfully say he doesn't know anything. My wife is in the same position—especially so, as she's a criminal prosecutor."

Abi nodded, noting Asher still hadn't looked at her.

"Regarding the tape," James said, "there's every possibility it's been edited. You might not have even been answering the questions we've been led to believe you were. I admit, I don't like the tone of your voice when you said, 'We'll see,' but again, we don't know the context. They could've been talking about IFRT coming to rescue you and that's why you sounded so confident. Samuel's team are analyzing the tape right now, and we'll know more tomorrow."

"Okay," Abi said quietly, even though she felt anything but okay.

Asher looked to her intently. "They couldn't take you from me, Abi, so this is the next best thing they can try. Every move against me has been to break me down, and that's exactly what this tape is trying to do. But I refuse to let it. I'll handle this, and I'll make the person behind this recording pay for it."

James looked to Abi and nodded in agreement with Asher.

With one last look between them, his eyes settled on Asher. Asher gave the slightest nod, and then James dismissed himself. The sound of the door closing seemed to echo through the rom.

"I don't blame you for what you said, Abi. I meant what I said—I understand and I will support you through this, even if there is public fallout. But right now, honestly, I just want to forget about it for an hour or two, and then I'll make a plan to deal with this tape." He rubbed his hands over his face. The dark circles beneath his eyes seemed to be growing by the minute, Abi noted sadly before standing.

She walked toward him, her heart beating in her chest. She stopped a step away from him and he reached out for her. She took his hands, wrapping them around her waist as she stepped forward. Their eyes locked. "I don't know what happened during that interrogation, but I know two things: you mean more to me than you'll ever know, and that wouldn't change if you weren't king. When we met, you weren't in line to be king. Being queen has never been a goal of mine. Even if that tape wasn't cut, I can only assume I had that attitude at the time because I was trying to throw them off. The situation I was in . . . I couldn't appear weak and afraid. And I knew the more valuable I was to you, the more they would punish me. I love you, Asher. If you walked away from your title tomorrow, I would walk with you—I need you to know that."

He pulled her into his lap and cupped her cheeks. "I do know that. I do," he said, locking his eyes on hers. "It's us against the world, Abi." He brushed his lips over hers.

She placed a sweet, lingering kiss on his lips. "Me and you . . . and Thomas Security," she added with a laugh.

"They help a little," Asher said, grinning. The sight of Asher beaming a full smile warmed her heart—it was mesmerizing.

He took her hand and ran a thumb over her knuckles, pausing on a ring finger. "I need to get you a ring," he said.

Abi smiled, but it didn't reach her eyes.

"What?" Asher asked quickly.

"Nothing," she said, shaking her head softly.

Asher raised an eyebrow expectantly.

"Maybe we should wait. I don't want you to put a ring on my

finger, announce our engagement, and then the voice recording is released to the public. It'll be a nightmare for you to deal with."

"Abi, this tape is probably going to be a nightmare regardless. It would be easier for me to deal with it if you have a ring on your finger," Asher said.

She pulled back, watching him carefully. "Do you think I'd walk away?" Santina's divorce rate was low—divorce happened, but it wasn't common. Couples tended to stick together and work it out. Abi had thought that the stigma of divorce might've been one of the main reasons—children included, of course—that her parents had stayed together after her father's liaison with Emilia.

"Abi, I would understand if you walked away at any time, but especially now," Asher said, his eyes pained. "There's every chance you're going to be heavily criticized in the media—and you'll have me to thank for that. Yes, you're William Bennett's daughter, but our relationship makes your story a front page feature. You will be unfairly criticized and I've seen what that can do to people." He looked away from her uncertainly.

"I'm not going anywhere," she said without hesitation. "When I said I would marry you, I meant it. I won't walk away when things get tough. You said we were forever, so put that ring on my finger! If I'm going to be unfairly criticized, I want the world to know I have your support, at least."

Asher pressed his lips to hers. "I will fight for you. Always."

ABI

Asher's tongue swept over hers with a hunger she hadn't felt in days. She wasn't grateful or happy for the fallout that was surely coming, but one thing was becoming very clear: Asher met every challenge. The more difficult the circumstances, the more he rose to meet them. She was proud to stand beside him—and proud to marry him. She just hoped he'd think the same of her in a few weeks' time.

Asher pulled back, leaning in his chair, a sly smirk on his lips.

"What?" Abi asked.

His eyes sparkled. "I just had the craziest idea."

Abi's eyes darted around like she expected his source of inspiration to jump out from behind him.

"Care to elaborate?" she asked, barely able to contain her smile—Asher's was contagious.

"I know exactly how to handle this," he said, his eyes far away but his words energized.

"Asher, communicate," Abi said gently, growing impatient.

Asher returned his attention to her. "I'm going to release the tape—on my terms."

Abi's mouth fell open. "Why would you do that? You don't even know what's on the rest of the recording?"

"It doesn't matter," Asher said, shaking his head. "The context is what matters. And if I explain it first, I get the chance to put the context in Santina's mind. Where's James?" he asked, his eyes landing on the door.

Asher picked up the phone. "Can you come in? . . . Thanks."

A moment later, James Thomas strode in with his signature swagger. "At your service," he said with a grin.

Abi looked between them, amazed at how relaxed two men in positions of such responsibility could be.

"I want to make a speech regarding the context of the tape of Abi. I'm going to handle this on my terms—not theirs," Asher said.

James looked ahead, his eyes thoughtful. A moment later, a spark lit in them and the corner of the lips turned up. "You're going to bring in the case we talked about, aren't you?"

"It's the perfect storm," Asher said with a tight smile.

Abi looked between them. "Can someone please fill me in?"

James looked to Asher, Asher shrugged. "It'll be better if you wait and see."

She raised an eyebrow. "This concerns me and my reputation, so I'd rather not wait and see."

Asher gave a reluctant sigh. "There's a case I asked James and Samuel to look into—a serious human-rights violation case. Accusations were made against the Adani royals but no one could ever find the evidence to link them to the crimes." He grinned. "Not until Samuel and his sidekicks came along."

"What were they accused of?" Abi asked, trying to recall all the major cases that had received publicity over the years. She could only think of one major case that had almost destroyed them.

Her jaw dropped and Asher nodded. "Correct."

"Asher," Abi said, her voice choking, "you better make damn sure you have enough evidence to accuse them of poisoning the poor people's water supply."

"You won't believe what Samuel found—"

Asher's phone rang before he could finish the sentence. Abi was unconsciously leaning in, her heart palpating with anticipation.

"King Asher," he answered.

Asher's face tightened as he listened to the person on the other end of the line.

James's eyes narrowed and focused on the desk like he was concentrating hard. Could he hear the conversation?

Abi looked to his ear but knew she wouldn't be able to see his earpiece even if he was wearing one.

Her attention was drawn back to Asher when he said, "That will be your biggest mistake," and hung up the phone.

Asher looked to James. "Set up the speech. I'll do it from the balcony."

James nodded and left without a word.

Abi looked to Asher expectantly.

He sighed heavily. "That was one of King Khalil's officials advising they will be moving forward with the takeover of the Lithe Ruins—Alistair's deal."

Abi chewed on her cheek. "This is a war, Asher, however you look at it."

"And I'm ready to fight," he said, his eyes locked on hers.

Abi searched his eyes, but she saw no hesitation. She nodded and said, "And I'll fight beside you."

She leaned in and kissed his forehead, letting her lips linger a second longer. Reluctantly, she pulled away.

"I'll leave you to concentrate and work on your speech," she said.

Abi walked toward the door, feeling Asher's eyes on hers. A nervousness bubbled in her chest. It wasn't that she didn't believe in Asher, or that she questioned what Samuel had found, but she knew there would be no going back after making a claim like the one Asher was going to make. This revelation would change the world, and it would change Santina forever.

She pressed her lips together as a question popped into her mind. Why had Asher asked Samuel to look into this virus specifically? She wondered if King Martin had thought them guilty but didn't have the evidence to back up such a claim. Or did he?

Her mind spun with questions she would never be able to answer. But maybe this long-thought-out planned revolt was about more than just power—perhaps it was about covering their dirty secrets. And if Asher exposed them, he would amplify the target on his back. If Adani secrets were exposed, they could still kill Asher as punishment; from what she knew about the Adani royals and their government officials, they were capable of every horrifying deed imaginable.

Abi was so lost in her thoughts she didn't hear her name being called, until it was clear from the tone that it wasn't the first time it had been yelled out.

And it took her a moment to realize who the voice belonged to.

She turned, surprised to face Alistair.

"Hi. I'm sorry, I was distracted by something," Abi said, watching Alistair carefully. Security stood beside her and she stole a sideways glance. They appeared relaxed.

Alistair didn't miss the sideways glance.

He sighed. "Can we talk for a few minutes—privately?"

"Uh . . ." Abi started, faltering. She was grateful when security spoke on her behalf.

"King Asher's order is for Abi to be watched at all times. The King and Rachel are the only two people she can see unsupervised."

A flicker of something passed through Alistair's eyes so quickly Abi wondered if she'd imagined it.

"Fine, can we talk with your security team?" he asked, mockingly.

"Sure," Abi said, despite it being the last thing she wanted to do.

Alistair eyed her a moment and then motioned to the door nearest them. Abi realized she'd never been inside that room—she'd never noticed it being there.

She looked to security again, two of whom entered first. Abi assumed they were scoping the room because when they emerged they nodded and motioned for her to enter.

When Abi walked in, she realized it was a large room with two desks. One was a mess with piles of paper and a dirty cup by the computer. The other was meticulously clean—everything in order so much so that it looked like it belonged in a display home.

Alistair sat on the edge of the messy desk. In that moment, his posture, even his eyes, looked like Asher.

"Asher and I swapped desks," he said, his voice dry. "This was his office . . . he shared it with Noah," he said, gesturing toward the clean desk.

Abi smiled sadly—now it made sense. She looked over the desk again, trying to imagine Noah there, chatting and laughing with Asher.

All but two security guards left the room. The two that remained stood back, against the walls. Their posture was rigid, like they were ready to pounce.

Abi just wanted to run from the room altogether.

"So . . ." Abi started, turning over her hands.

Alistair drew a long breath and exhaled heavily. "Look, I just want to apologize. I don't have anything against you in particular, it's just . . ." His voice trailed off and he looked uncomfortable as he searched for the right words. "There's a long history of rivalry between Asher and me that complicates our relationship . . . and therefore my attitude toward you."

Abi raised her eyebrow at his choice of word. *Rivalry.* She wasn't sure Asher thought there had ever been rivalry on his behalf, but she wasn't going to speak for him. She just wanted this over with.

"Thank you," she said cautiously.

He nodded. She noticed he couldn't meet her eyes, but she didn't know what to make of that. Was he lying? Or was he just having a hard time apologizing?

"Why now?" Abi asked, her curiosity winning the war over getting out of the office.

Alistair's eyes widened slightly, indicating he was surprised. "Because I owe Asher more than I can ever repay him. So, if that means supporting his relationship with you, then that's what I need to do."

Abi looked at him like he'd grown two heads. Who was this version of Alistair?

"How many siblings do you have?" Alistair asked.

"Three sisters," Abi responded, unsure where he was going with this.

"Are you the most successful of them?" Alistair asked.

"Um . . ." Abi said, unsure how to answer that. "We all took very different paths, I really don't think you could compare us."

Alistair gave an odd smile. "You're lucky then, and because of that I can't expect you to understand. But growing up, and even now, everyone —our parents, the media, our enemies—compared Asher and me." He looked at his feet and seemed to struggle with his words. "I have felt like a failure my entire life," he said, still looking down. "That's why I did what I did and took the drugs—I wanted to numb the pain, the embarrassment. But in reality what I was doing was just securing my fate as a fuckup."

Abi stood there awkwardly—she didn't know how to respond. "Well I know for sure there are people who believe in you. People make mistakes, Alistair, but that doesn't mean there's no hope for the future."

He chuckled and Abi couldn't tell if it was he was embarrassed or mocking her.

"You two are going to be a match made in heaven," he said like he couldn't believe it. He gave a slight shake of his head. "Anyway," he said, his voice clearer, "I just wanted to apologize and let you know I don't have a problem with you, and I'm not going to hurt you or anyone in this palace. I have a temper, but I just like to yell and shout at people. I don't kill."

Abi raised an eyebrow. "I never thought you did," she said, but not for the reasons she wanted him to believe. At one point she thought he might've been the mastermind behind her abduction, but never did she actually think he did the dirty work himself.

He looked at her, blinking, like he was stunned.

"I need to get going. I have a few phone calls to make," Abi said quickly.

"Sure," Alistair said, his face impassive once more.

Abi nodded, then began to walk toward the door.

"Abi, I have something for you . . . think of it as a welcome gift," he said before pulling out an abstract painting of Santina. Abi knew the artist—she'd even looked at the painting in an exhibition.

"Alistair, I can't take this," Abi said, her eyes going wide. "It's an incredible painting and very expensive."

Alistair gave a lopsided grin. "Don't tell anyone," he said with a laugh, and Abi felt a twinge of amusement considering they were being constantly watched, "but I bought it one night on a bender. I could never find quite the right place for it and then I learned you'd set up an office. I know the room, and this would be perfect." His smile faltered. "Please, take it. Every time I look at it, it brings back memories I'd rather forget. But that's my own doing."

Abi weighed her options and decided to accept the gift. "Thank you, I really appreciate it," she said, and meant it. "It's an incredible piece."

Alistair gave a smile as he handed over the painting. Abi didn't know if he was happy or sad.

Maybe he was both.

ASHER

Asher looked at the telephone, wondering if this was the hardest call he'd ever have to make. He prayed it was, because he couldn't imagine anything worse.

Asher's eyes darted to the crystal clock. He'd been procrastinating for the last half hour. If he didn't pick up the phone now, he'd run out of time—and there was no way he'd be able to make this speech without making this call first.

He exhaled a sigh that sounded like a groan and picked up the telephone.

His uncle answered on the first ring. "Hello."

"Uncle, this is Asher," he said.

"Asher? Hi," he responded casually. "How are you?"

"Not good, I'm afraid. I need to tell you something, and I want to tell you in advance that I'm sorry. Are you home? Is Aunty there with you?" Asher asked.

"Yes we're home; I'm sitting at my desk. Is it your mother? Is she okay?" he asked, firing off the questions.

"She's fine . . . I'm calling about Troy," Asher said.

There was a pause before he spoke. "Is he there with you? We've been trying to reach him for the past few days."

"Yes, he's here. In the cells," Asher said.

"In the cells? What are you talking about?" The tone of his voice turned dark in seconds.

"Troy has been implicated in my father's murder and in the murder of Noah," Asher said gently.

"What? Asher, this is ridiculous! We're talking about your friend—your cousin—your own blood!"

Asher straightened, physically bracing himself. "He did not care that my father was his own blood when he orchestrated his murder. He has been posturing under an alias, Martin Snider, who is responsible for the deaths and leading a revolt—"

"He is not Martin Snider! How can you accuse him of this?" his uncle's voice boomed through the line.

"He has admitted his involvement," Asher said defensively. He hadn't even told him the worst news yet.

"No, he's told you what you wanted to hear so that you didn't hurt him—because I know your security team, Asher, and I know exactly what they're capable of and how they operate."

"Uncle, I know this is hard, and I know he's your son, but he murdered the king and Noah. This can't go unpunished," Asher said, keeping his voice calm and unwavering.

A long pause followed.

"What are you going to do?" he asked, a violent tone to his voice.

Asher squeezed his eyes shut. "He will be executed. I wanted to give you the courtesy of finding out from me, rather than from the media."

The pause that followed was so long, Asher thought the call had been disconnected.

"You're making a huge mistake," he eventually said.

"I wish that were true. I wish it was all a misunderstanding, but it's not," Asher said quietly.

"If you're wrong, Asher, can you live with the fact that you killed an innocent man? Your cousin, no less?"

"I will do what needs to be done. Being a blood relative doesn't mean you get away with murder. If it were anyone else, I would execute them too. Troy doesn't get to escape that because of who he is," Asher said, his voice rising, not backing down.

"We will not forgive you for this," his uncle said ominously before hanging up.

Asher stared at his desk as he listened to the beeping in his ear.

Finally he hung up the phone and rested his face in his hands.

What else had he expected? Troy was his son, and there was nothing Asher could have said to make that news any better.

Asher shook his head, groaning. He didn't look up when his door opened, but he knew it was James.

"Interesting response," Asher said. "He didn't ask who Martin Snider was, and he seemed more composed than I would've expected for a father just learning his son is to be executed."

James nodded. "He also said they've been trying to reach Troy, yet there's no phone calls to Troy's mobile from any of the numbers—cell phones or landlines. Samuel just checked."

He blew out a long breath as he tipped his head back, trying to think through the pressure that seemed to be weighing on him more heavily each day.

"You don't need to give the name today," James said, surprising him. "Just say that the king's killer will be executed in two days' time."

Asher shook his head. "If I don't say the name, they'll think I'm hiding something and we don't really know for sure." Asher groaned. "This is a fucking mess!" he said, standing and grabbing his notes. He didn't have time to deal with this right now—Santina was waiting for him.

James and Asher walked side by side with a security team behind them.

The curtains were drawn across the window of the balcony. As they approached, the curtains opened and Asher stepped forward before he gave himself a chance to hesitate.

He looked over the crowd—one far larger than he'd expected given the short notice. He looked at their individual faces—the faces of the people he had to protect. He could only do that with his enemies eliminated.

"Santina," Asher started and the crowd cheered. "Today is an important day. Today is the day we stand up for those who couldn't fight for themselves."

A hushed murmur flowed through the crowd like a wave in the ocean.

"Recently I received a voice recording—one taken while Abi was in captivity, while she was drugged and under unfathomable stress. This recording was not given to me as a gift, it was given to me with a blackmail threat.

"It is no secret that for many years—until she was taken hostage— Abi was the leader of the International Female Rescue Team: a team known for their daring rescues, for going to places where other rescue teams wouldn't dare," he said, raising a cheer, if a short-lived one, from the audience.

"Unfortunately, on missions like those, there is the risk of casualties in order to retrieve the hostages—the innocent women and children taken from their villages who are violently raped and abused multiple times each day, every day.

"This voice recording discusses one of these missions, and in the context of the recording, it would be easy to forget the perilous dangers to the IFRT staff and the hostages they are rescuing. If someone came into your home and attacked you, would you hesitate to kill them to rescue your family?"

The crowd was silent, but Asher saw a few nodding heads.

"I ask you to remember this if you listen to the recording over the next few days, because I will not be blackmailed. I will release the tape to Santina, because neither I nor Abi have anything to hide. I will not surrender to those who are trying to hurt us—to our enemies!"

At this the crowd cheered again, this time louder.

"Sometimes our enemies are from other kingdoms, but sometimes they are from Santina. I didn't want to believe it myself . . . but the investigation into King Martin's death has revealed that to be true."

The crowd looked over their shoulders and at one another, suddenly fearful.

"The king's slayer has been captured," Asher said, projecting a strong voice. "And he will be executed in two days' time. No one is allowed to commit murder in Santina and get away with it. No one. And no one will blackmail Santina and get away with it! Those who are attempting to blackmail me should make sure they aren't hiding any dirty secrets, because I will expose them to the world," Asher said, looking directly at the media camera below.

"I will be releasing further details about the king's slayer within the next twenty-four hours. Santina, I promised you I would punish the person responsible for murdering your king . . . and that day is coming."

The crowd roared so loud that for a moment it almost took Asher aback. The crowd was ready for blood, and he was glad it wasn't his they were cheering for.

King Asher.
Hail King Asher.

REED

Reed ignored the roar of the crowd and narrowed his gaze. His head had been pounding since he left the hospital, but he refused to sit in the palace and do nothing. He looked through his scope to the people below. He had no intention of shooting anyone—not yet—but he was looking for a familiar face.

"Reed, can you see your friend?" Samuel asked.

"Negative," he responded.

"Hmm," Samuel mused, but he didn't sound surprised. Neither was Reed, given that Asher had spoken to him and given him warning minutes before his speech. But if he was here, Reed knew he wasn't in the crowd to hear what the king had to say. It was very possible he was there to silence the king.

Nonetheless, Reed continued to scan the faces of the crowd. He'd expected them to disperse once Asher stepped back inside, but the crowd lingered, talking amongst themselves. There was an energy, an excitement that Reed hadn't seen before. The crowd seemed at one with each other, creating a vibration that was palpable—almost visible.

That troubled Reed.

Santina was growing tired of their country being threatened, and they wanted blood. Soon they wouldn't care whose blood it was—as long as someone was paying. If Asher wasn't careful, they might turn on him.

He did a double-take when he thought he saw a familiar face, but it turned out to be a false alarm. He kept scanning, confident that between all of the men Thomas Security had on the rooftops, no one would pass by undetected.

It took over an hour for the crowd to disperse. Finally, Reed lowered his weapon.

"Negative," Reed said. "I'm packing up."

"Copy," Samuel responded.

Similar calls continued to come in from the team. Reed was disappointed, even though he hadn't had high expectations of seeing Asher's uncle there—and even lower expectations of him doing something desperate to try to take out the king.

Reed knew that was a good thing, but the uncertainty of this case was troubling. Every time they felt like they were close, things took a turn—usually for the worse.

"Regroup at the palace. I want a meeting," James said.

"Copy," Reed responded as he slung his kit over his shoulder and walked toward the stairwell. His senses were on full alert as he descended the stairs and walked out to the waiting car. He was inside and on his way to the palace without incident.

Reed exhaled a long breath.

He used the quiet time to churn the facts around in his mind. He couldn't shake the feeling that they were missing something. This case was like a giant three-dimensional puzzle with moving parts. Every piece had to fit.

His mind was no clearer by the time he arrived. He went straight to James's newly acquired office, passing the kitchen as he did. His eyes darted left, to the lone figure at the table by the window. He couldn't make out any of her features—she was nothing more than a silhouette—but he knew it was Rachel.

His legs stopped but he forced himself to move forward. He was working a case and could not afford to be distracted. James had given him a gift sending him to Santina; he'd dreamed about taking a case like this for years. He had one shot now, and he wouldn't blow it.

Leave it. Keep walking.

Ten guys, including James, were sitting around the table when he walked in. They nodded toward him and James pulled out the chair beside him, motioning for him to sit.

"I'm worried about that crowd," Reed said quietly.

James sighed. "Me too," he admitted as the screen on the wall activated and Samuel, Deacon, and Cami waved hello.

Samuel got straight to business. "We've run full forensics on the tape Asher received. It hasn't been edited. Abi was answering the questions she was asked," he said.

"That's not what I wanted to hear," James muttered.

"No, but it's the truth—it's one continuous stream. In light of that, what are your thoughts?" Deacon asked.

James groaned. "I think she was under extreme pressure and in all honesty, she didn't actually say anything that damaging, it's just that in the context the average person will view it in. Even with Asher's forewarning and explanation, this will go two ways: it will be a public-relations nightmare for Asher, or Abi could be heralded as a revolutionary and the tape could be a gift from his enemies."

"I think the best thing he can do is give the media something else to focus on," Deacon said. "He needs to make a big move—something to draw attention away from Abi. He should execute Troy, and do it fast."

"He needs to make that move anyway. Santina will grow restless if they think he's moving too slowly," James said, then added, "They're already restless and hungry for blood."

Everyone around the table nodded in agreement.

"And he needs more money," Samuel said. "He's not moving fast enough on securing aid. I know he's had a lot to deal with, but without money to feed his people, his life is going to become a lot harder—especially if he is criticized for Abi's tape."

"He has a meeting with William Bennett this afternoon," James said. "Any talk of Martin Snider?"

Samuel shook his head. "I haven't intercepted anything, which suggests that our assumption that Troy is Martin Snider is correct."

"That, or the real Martin Snider wants us to think that and is keeping a very low profile right now. I'm going to speak to Troy again tonight. We'll see if he offers up anything of interest," James said.

"So, the game plan is what?" Deacon asked, getting the meeting back on track.

"One: Asher needs to secure funding, starting immediately, because those deals will take time to set up and negotiate," James replied. "Two: While he's doing that, he needs to make his next move . . . whatever that might be. Three: While Asher is busy with all of the above, we need to find out who sent that recording. I've fingerprinted it and Samuel is running the searches."

"No matches yet," Samuel said. "The address on the back doesn't actually exist, but each post office in Santina has its own stamp, so we know where it was sent from. I'm running facial recognition software from the CCTV footage of three cameras in the area to see if anyone interesting pops up. I think it's highly unlikely we'll be able to pick that up, but until we get a better lead I think it's worth investigating."

"Agreed," James confirmed. "We've had worse odds before."

"How is Asher's headspace right now?" Deacon asked, looking directly at Jesse. "Executing his cousin—someone he once trusted—and being blackmailed is enough to make him spiral out of control."

"He's okay," Jesse said simply. "He's coping, and I don't think we can ask for much more than that right now. Asher will do what needs to be done." There was no doubt in his voice.

"An execution is the best move he can make right now," James said. "It was exactly the same tactic Vince used by killing his son when his power and control was threatened. It's a very effective message."

Deacon nodded and Reed wasn't surprised by his next words.

"There's something bothering me about Troy's comment about Noah," Deacon said. "Troy said Noah didn't tell Asher about the revolt because he was trying to protect him, but that's very contradictory. If he was trying to protect him, if Asher had known and had gone to his father, things might've turned out very differently for all of them."

"What is your gut feeling about what Noah knew?" James asked his brother.

"Well, he knew about Alistair's fling and even had photos of the woman and child. So, how did he get them? They didn't come through his email; Samuel has already checked. More than likely, someone physically passed the images to him. So, why didn't he go to Asher? It doesn't make sense—unless he wasn't sure that Troy was Martin Snider. Troy is definitely involved, but is he actually Martin Snider? We haven't confirmed that, and that is something that definitely needs to be confirmed before Asher executes him."

"Well, there's one way to find out," Reed said with a crooked grin.

James wiggled his eyebrows, and Samuel sighed and shook his head.

"Come on," James said, and Reed grinned—watching James Thomas in an interrogation was Reed's favorite kind of movie to watch.

They strode from the office down to the "cells." They were quite different from the cells at Thomas Security—clearly, the palace had never intended on having many guests.

The rooms were bare, with little more than concrete and drywall. They had limited surveillance, no sound-proofing, and no drains for blood.

But, they did the job.

"What's your gut feeling?" James asked as they walked.

Reed's eyebrows lifted in surprise. "I think his father is Martin Snider. I think Troy is Martin Snider's lackey—a son who thought he'd be next in line for the throne once his father took power."

James nodded thoughtfully but didn't respond.

He entered the cell first; Reed followed closely behind, before closing the door and locking it. When he turned around, Troy looked at them with wide eyes, his face obscured by sutures and bandages.

What a waste of time that was.

"What do you want?" Troy asked quickly.

"I want to know who Martin Snider is," James said simply, crossing his arms and leaning against the wall. Reed recognized the posture as one James used when he wanted to send a message: *You don't threaten me, and you should not fuck with me.*

Troy looked at the floor and visibly swallowed, then looked up with conviction in his eyes.

"I'm Martin Snider," he finally said.

"But you're not," James said, sounding bored.

Troy straightened. "What are you talking about? I am Martin Snider."

Reed watched him closely for all the signs that he might be lying—he noted how quickly he blinked, if his shoulders were tense, if his jaw was grinding, if his fingers had a subtle tremor.

It was hard to distinguish between a nervous person and a liar during an interrogation, but there was a very subtle difference, and that difference changed for each person.

Troy's hands were steady and his body relaxed, but it was the fire in his eyes that gave him away. It's easier to be courageous and to lie for someone else than it is to do it for yourself—especially when that person is someone you love.

"Do you know how I know you're lying?" James asked, taking a step forward and then another. He was like a lion, moving in on his prey. James reached for his back pocket and Reed had to force himself to smother his smirk.

When James waved his scalpel in front of Troy, he started yelling, "I'm talking, I'm talking!"

"But you're saying all the wrong things," James said, his voice menacing, his patience clearly long worn out.

"I'm Martin Snider!" Troy said. "I've been orchestrating this all. It's me! Kill me now, I don't care! Just get it over with."

Reed shook his head.

Rookie mistake, Troy.

James turned around. "We're done," he said and Reed nodded in agreement.

The moment the door closed behind them, James said, "Find his father."

"On it," Reed said.

Troy's biggest mistake had been to show them he was ready to die. It wasn't him; he was covering for someone else.

The problem with someone resolved to dying was that it made it difficult to get them to talk, and Reed and James knew that Troy would die before he gave up his father explicitly—so they would only be wasting precious moments, because every minute his father was alone was another minute for him to disappear.

Reed ran through the hallway, grabbed a set of keys, and revved the engine.

"Samuel, tell me where he is," Reed said as he put the car in reverse and planted his foot on the accelerator.

"He's at his home," Samuel replied quickly. *"Your backup will be right behind you. Go!"*

ASHER

Asher forced a smile as his mother entered his office. "Hey," he said, sounding tired even to his own ears.

"What's wrong?" she asked immediately.

Asher sighed heavily. "Take a seat. I have some news . . . and you're not going to like it."

She sat in the chair opposite him and the irony of the moment made him pause. So many times she'd sat in that very seat across from her husband, and now she was sitting across from her son while he explained who killed her husband.

"Is this about your father's murderer?" she asked.

"Yes," Asher said, clasping his hands on his desk. "Father's murder, Noah's murder, Abi's kidnapping. They're all connected."

Asher had refrained from telling her too much too soon—he was worried he might only disappoint her if the team couldn't capture the killer—and now they were going to have not one, but two.

"I saw your speech," she said, and Asher detected the tone in her voice. "And then I received a call from your uncle. You should've come to me with this, Asher."

Asher nodded. "There wasn't time. And, unfortunately, Troy isn't the only one involved."

Her eyebrows lifted but she showed no joy at that news. "I want them all punished," she said, her voice tight.

"We think—we're sure—that Uncle himself is involved. A team is on the way to his house now and they'll pick him up and bring him back here to interrogate him."

Emilia face turned two shades whiter. "I couldn't understand Troy's involvement, but I tried to rationalize it telling myself that your father and Troy were never particularly close. But his own brother?"

"I know," Asher said. "Troy said that our family was incapable of leading Santina, that we were ruining it, and so they had no option but to take matters into their own hands."

Her mouth fell open. "Your father was dealt one challenge after another and Santina didn't fall. We did the best we could—the best anyone could!"

Asher took her hand. "I know. I'm not agreeing with them, I'm telling you that's their justification."

She shook her head like she couldn't believe it. "How sure are you? You can't undo this, Asher. This is going to change our family, and Santina's legacy, forever."

"There's little doubt in my mind. Thomas Security thought right from the start this was done by someone close—close enough to our staff and to us. When I learned about the succession change, I asked Father why he didn't choose Troy. Father said he was too ambitious," Asher said, looking at his mother. "I keep wondering if Father knew more than he told us, or if it was a gut feeling? But either way, that gut feeling was correct."

Emilia pressed a finger to her temple. "He never mentioned anything to me. He would've if he was concerned," she said, her voice strained.

"Maybe he didn't have the chance," Asher said quietly.

Emilia looked up, her eyes glistening. "Are you going to execute them both?"

"Yes," Asher said without hesitation. "It's not what I want, but what choice do I have? If it was anyone else they would be executed. I won't make excuses for them—this was well planned, and they knew the risks."

Emilia nodded. "Despite it all, I feel for Grace."

"She's being investigated too," Asher cautioned. "But even if she's not involved, she only has her husband and son to blame for this."

"Do they have any evidence against her?" Emilia asked.

"No. Nothing," Asher said slowly. "But maybe they simply haven't found it yet."

Emilia sighed, leaning back in her chair. She shook her head softly. "She was the first person to comfort me after Martin's death," she said, rubbing her temples. "I doubt she'll want my comfort after all of this."

"Well, that's her family's fault, not ours," Asher said firmly. "They took two lives—lives they had no right to take. And then blackmailed me and killed hundreds of innocent Santinians. They don't get to live now. They're not even sorry, Troy has shown no remorse."

Emilia looked to him with soft eyes. "I wish your father could see you now. He believed in you, but I think you've surpassed even his expectations. I wish he could've grown old with me, seeing the full potential of his family."

Asher smiled sadly. "I like to think he and Noah are watching over us. Sometimes I swear I hear Father's voice."

"I talk to him all the time," Emilia admitted, her eyes far away.

Asher reached for her hand and gave it a squeeze.

But the moment was interrupted when the screen activated and security footage began playing.

"That's their house," Emilia said.

Asher nodded. "The teams have arrived."

Emilia bit her lip, then looked away. "I'm going to leave you to it," she said, standing. "Make decisions you can sleep with at night," she told him simply. "That's the motto your father lived by."

Asher only nodded, and when Emilia closed the door behind her, he didn't hesitate before returning his attention to the screen.

"In position."

Asher recognized Reed's voice immediately. He wondered again how Reed was upright and back on the field so quickly after being hospitalized.

"In position," James said.

Asher looked at the house, his mind spinning, his stomach churning. His uncle lived in an old palace, one built almost a hundred years ago. Previously a military command base, it had been upgraded and refurbished before Asher was born and again more recently.

Asher paused, realizing he'd missed the first sign that something wasn't right. He'd noticed it the moment he'd walked into their house after the most recent renovations—he'd dismissed it as odd and hadn't given it any more thought; but their house had been renovated to look like the palace—same colors, same style. Asher tried to recall when Aunty and Uncle had done the renovations. Three years ago? Maybe four?

How long had Martin Snider been planning this revolt?

Asher's jaw ground together. Martin Snider was going to be very disappointed when his long-planned efforts to destroy Asher's family were exposed.

"Three, two, one!"

Asher subconsciously leaned forward and watched the footage.

A second passed . . . and then another . . .

He held his breath, waiting to see what was happening, but no one appeared to be moving.

Then Asher straightened, his breath catching in his throat as he saw the front of the building explode into a fiery blaze.

"Go!" James said.

The footage blurred as the men ran toward the palace. The blurring footage was making Asher nervous, and he returned his attention to the front of the house. No one was rushing to put the flames out.

He narrowed his eyes, squinting to see clearly.

But he couldn't see anyone at all.

Asher knew if his palace was on fire, security would be out front immediately doing damage control.

So where was everyone?

REED

Reed's heart stammered in his chest and his legs felt like dead weights. He reached the house and took a moment to catch his breath, then leaned forward, resting his hands on his knees while his teammates covered him.

"You okay?" one asked.

"Yeah, just give me a minute," Reed said, breathing hard.

When James had asked him if he felt good enough to go on this mission tonight, he'd answered honestly: Yes, he felt fine. He'd even felt fine in the gym this afternoon.

But now his head felt fuzzy, and he felt like he had a ton of weights strapped to his legs.

Reed drew a long breath and straightened.

Mind over matter.

It wasn't quite that simple, but he needed to lead his team in and if he had to back out now, it would compromise their position.

"No one's come out to attend to the blaze."

Reed nodded to his teammate. "As we expected. They've seen what we're capable of, so they'll retreat. Let's find them before they escape."

Reed straightened, his head feeling clearer now that he could breathe again. He crept forward, keeping his shoulder against the wall.

His eyes darted from point to point, his mind hyper aware of the danger they were in. A mission like this was always risky because they didn't know the property, and their enemy did—but a disadvantage did not mean defeat, and hopefully they'd caught their enemies unprepared.

He looked up at a security camera. He saw the red light, indicating it was recording. Reed smiled and waved, feeling a childlike glee of satisfaction.

I'm coming for you, Uncle.

He ran forward, light on his feet once more. He had ten men behind him and six other teams were coming in. Soon they'd have the property secured.

"Reed, move in straight away." James's command came through loud and clear.

"Copy," Reed said still smiling. It was his favorite command to hear; he never was one for idle surveillance. Reed knew it was necessary but he always grew restless with anticipation. James knew this about him and always gave him the first team to lead in. That came with additional risks, though, because statistically the first team in was the first team to die.

But not tonight, Reed told himself. *Not tonight.*

Reed tested the door handle and paused when it moved. Why would the door be unlocked? That was either a mistake by a purely incompetent security team—which Reed didn't think was the case—or they wanted this door to be an entry point.

The temptation to enter was an enticing as fresh blood to a vampire, but Reed held back.

He held his palm up to his team, signaling them to hold.

"James, the door is unlocked. I think it's a trap," Reed said.

"*Move to Plan B*," James said without hesitation.

And that was one of the things Reed respected most about his boss: if one of the team had a bad feeling about something or raised a concern, it wasn't questioned. Entry through this door was ideal given the palace layout and it gave them the most advantage points, but James would reroute their strategy if anyone raised a concern.

"Copy," Reed said, already running. He spotted another security camera and raised his pistol, shattering it. He was no longer in the mood for pleasantries.

Reed saw the door ahead but as they ran past the window, something caught his eye. The drapes were slightly open, as if someone had been looking out, and Reed saw a female run past. She seemed to be on her own—strange.

If the palace was being attacked, their security should've gathered everyone together.

Reed supposed it could've been a security officer, but the posture of the woman suggested otherwise. She was too hunched, too small.

"James, Plan C. I'm going in the window. I think I saw the aunt," Reed said quickly.

"Copy," James responded as Reed's elbow smashed the glass. He had one hand through the window, reaching for the lock when the glass panel beside his arm shattered.

Reed ducked, shielding his body. He grabbed a mirror from his pocket and raised it up, but the room was empty.

He raised his pistol, firing blindly into the room to give him a chance to stand and get inside. They needed to move fast, because this palace had underground tunnels like Asher's palace and there was a chance they were already too late.

"Target identified!" James shouted a second before gunfire drowned out his voice. Reed spun around in time to see ten men storming toward them, and he dove behind the couch before crawling forward, his pulse whooshing through his ears. He paused, listening to every sound in the room. The plush carpet made it difficult to hear their footsteps but Reed caught the shadows cast by the dim floor lamp. He watched them closely and when the footsteps became a faint, padded sound on the carpet, Reed rolled out and fired straight into the feet of the men. He sprung up, ignoring his protesting body, then fired shots into their chests, making sure they didn't get up again.

He caught the look of one of his team members.

"What?" Reed asked.

The man smirked. "I still don't know how you move like that."

Reed raised an eyebrow but he didn't have time to ask more questions.

"Reed! We're cornered! South wing!" James said.

Reed's breath caught in his throat—James never considered himself cornered until he was facing death.

"Go!" Reed shouted, raising a hand to motion his team forward as he sprinted ahead.

He ran the length of the long hallway, his weapon raised, his senses on high alert. His teammates were a step behind him, and as they turned the next corner, he heard gunfire.

Reed slowed as they approached the origin of the sound, and it took him a second to realize the full extent of what he was looking at.

James had five men with him, all backed into the corner of an industrial kitchen, most of which had been set alight. Flames licked the cabinetry, and a smoky haze reduced visibility. Reed followed the direction of their weapons, spotting the teams they were firing at. He couldn't see the men from his position, but he thought there had to be at least twenty men to corner James—at least.

We've had worse odds, Reed thought as he breathed in the choking, thick air.

What is with these guys and fires?

Reed shook his head. He was pissed off now—he'd inhaled enough smoke to last him the next ten years and he was done.

He pulled a grenade from his back pocket. "Hold!" he commanded his team as he lifted his T-shirt, pulling it over his nose and mouth as he stepped forward. The smoky haze had its advantages, though—for one, it made Reed a little less visible.

"Keep them occupied," Reed said to James as he moved toward the kitchen. Once he'd rounded the corner, he saw the men firing at James and his team. Three clusters, at least thirty men, if not more.

Reed cocked a smile as he pulled the pin on a grenade and launched it.

"Down!" he screamed a second before the grenade landed, lighting up the kitchen.

Reed sprung to his feet and sprinted forward, firing. He'd dropped his T-shirt and the first full inhalation of smoke knocked the oxygen from his lungs. He gasped, feeling like he was choking, but he ignored his burning lungs and fired. The sooner he killed these guys, the sooner he could get out.

James burst through the haze, his weapon unloading on the small group of men still standing. But now the tables had turned and the men who hadn't been blown up were backed into a corner. However, Reed was not in the mood for taking prisoners—except for one.

Using the wall as a shield, he pulled his T-shirt up over his nose and mouth again.

James was standing against the wall on the other side of him and Reed didn't miss the look he cast him.

"Are you okay?"

"Yeah," Reed said as a cough caught in his throat, exposing his lie.

James looked over his shoulder then something flickered through his eyes. He pulled a grenade, launched it, and Reed ducked down, shielding his head with his hands. The house shook with a deafening bang and they surged forward again. Reed couldn't see anything through the wall of flames, but there was no return gunfire.

James leapt over the flames and Reed heard two shots fired.

He suppressed another cough.

"Jackson, get Reed out of here," James commanded.

"I'm fine!" Reed said.

"Jackson! Get him out!" James commanded and Reed felt a hand on his elbow.

He sighed. He wouldn't disobey a direct order from James, and neither would Jackson. They retreated, leaving the way they'd come.

As soon as they were out of the kitchen and away from the smoke, Reed's lungs seemed to open up and he could breathe properly again.

"Look at that," Jackson said, pointing to a blood trail on the floor.

"It's on our way out," Reed said, trying to convince Jackson—and himself—that they weren't disobeying James's order by taking a detour.

They quickened their pace following the blood trail, which became more obvious and the blood stains less defined. Looking at them,

Reed assumed someone had been hit in the leg and they'd started dragging that foot.

And then the trail stopped. Reed looked to the closest door and motioned toward it. Reed and Jackson stood on either side, and Reed pressed his ear to the wall, listening. When he heard nothing, he reached for the door handle and turned it, then kicked the door open before immediately flattening his back against the wall.

A bullet flew past him so close that Reed swore he heard it cutting through the air.

His heart pounded against his ribs and he touched his cheek and ear, but there was no blood.

Reed waited, signaling for Jackson to hold. He strained to hear, but there was no movement inside, so he inched forward—just as another gun shot rang out. Reed jolted back, analyzing his next move. He didn't want to use a grenade because he'd inhaled enough smoke already, and he wanted a clear view of what he was walking into.

He pulled out the next best thing: a flashbang.

Reed held it up to show Jackson and he nodded.

Reed angled his body and launched it inside. To his surprise, it made a thud—like it was hitting a wall—before it released a bang.

Reed moved fast, but he'd only taken two steps inside when he realized what had happened.

He kicked the pistol from the man's hands as light flooded the closet.

Asher's uncle sat with his back against the wall and a puddle of blood underneath his leg. When the man looked up at him and disgust filled his eyes, Reed realized the man could still see—somehow he'd avoided looking at the flashbang when it had gone off.

Reed smiled wide, baring his teeth. "Hello, Uncle," he said, pointing his weapon at the man's chest.

ASHER

*L*ike his son, Uncle showed no sign of remorse.

How do you murder your own brother and not feel remorse?

Asher exhaled a shaky breath as Reed cuffed his uncle and hauled him upright. He returned his attention to the camera footage that was linked to James Thomas. He was running through the tunnels—why? Was he simply eliminating the last of Uncle's men? Or was he looking for something?

Or someone?

"Clear."

"Clear."

"Clear."

"Samuel, what are they looking for?" Asher asked.

"Your Aunty. Reed thought he saw her in the house earlier," Samuel said.

He continued to watch the security footage but with each minute that passed, Asher's body relaxed a little. Eventually he leaned back in his chair, crossing his arms over his chest.

James's team searched all the tunnels and went back through the house, but Aunty was nowhere to be found.

Asher ran his palms over his face.

"Bring them to me," Asher said when James ordered all men to exit the house.

Asher picked up the telephone and dialed the palace doctor.

"Good evening, Your Majesty," he said, but then quickly corrected himself. "Good evening, Asher."

Asher supposed he was so used to using the formal title as he had done for the past twenty or more years that he did so without thinking.

"Evening. We will be needing some morphine tonight. Can you arrange it as soon as possible?"

"Of course. How much will you be needing, Asher?" the doctor asked, his voice wary.

"Enough to kill two adult men," Asher said, his voice tight.

There was a long pause at the other end. "Asher, I can't provide that."

"It's an order. The two men responsible for murdering King Martin and Noah will be executed tonight," Asher said.

They were lucky they would be executed with a hit of morphine, but it wasn't about the method for Asher—it was the psychological torture that would come with it.

"Of course," the doctor said, but he still sounded unsure.

"Thank you," Asher said before hanging up. He only needed the doctor to get the supplies, because apparently James Thomas was good at inserting intravenous lines and he was very willing to help.

Asher asked Samuel to turn off the screens and he left his office. He walked the hallways to his new living quarters, the room he was sharing with Abi, but something about the palace felt different tonight. There seemed to be less shadows, less imaginary whispers. Asher was sure it was all in his mind, but bringing his father's and Noah's murderers to justice gave him a sense of peace—two less killers on the streets of Santina and two less people aiming at his back. He'd expected to feel a slither of angst when this time came, but Asher didn't feel any angst or regret at all. He felt victorious and the fact that they were blood relatives made it even more important to do this.

Abi wasn't in the quarters when he entered so he went straight to the bathroom and showered. He didn't linger; he didn't need to wash away any dirty feelings today. Asher was surprisingly calm.

He changed into a clean pair of jeans and a white T-shirt and checked his reflection in the mirror. Fifty percent of his wardrobe was comprised of white business shirts or T-shirts, but tonight he felt different wearing white. White was a symbol of purity, and tonight he would take a major step forward in purifying Santina of the evil that had infiltrated it.

He walked down to the cells and waited patiently for the teams to arrive. Initially he sat with the security team before deciding to pay his cousin a visit. It was the first time he'd spoken to Troy alone since he'd been captured.

When Asher entered the cell, Troy was sitting on the cell floor with his back against the bed. His face was a composition of stitches and even though Asher had known he'd been stitched up, it was still shocking to see.

Troy looked like something out of a horror movie. Asher had asked the doctor why he had stitched Troy's face back up, given that his death was imminent, and the doctor had said, *"It's best we keep him free of infection... I thought you might like him lucid."*

Asher hadn't known whether to laugh or cry at that response—and he wondered again what people thought of him now. What did they think he was capable of?

He wanted them—his enemies—to ask themselves that every hour of every day. Because if they didn't know what he was capable of, they couldn't predict his next move, and that gave him power.

Troy didn't look his way when Asher entered. He wondered if Troy knew it was him, or if he refused to look at anyone who entered his cell.

"Your father is on his way to see you," Asher said, keeping his voice neutral and casual.

That caused Troy's head to turn toward him.

"I wanted to give you the chance to say goodbye to him," Asher continued, watching his cousin carefully.

"How kind of you," Troy answered mockingly.

Asher raised an eyebrow. "That's more than you gave me. You took Noah's life, and then my father's, and didn't give me a chance to say goodbye to either of them. The same would've been true for Abi and my mother if your plan hadn't failed."

It wasn't what Troy said, but it was the look in his eye. He appeared victorious, but he was in no position to be.

"Do you know what happens to a truck going downhill when the brakes fail, Asher?" Troy asked, but he didn't give Asher a chance to respond. He continued, "The driver realizes they've failed, but it's too late to stop it. The truck is already in motion and there's nothing you can do but sit and watch the wreck that's about to happen. That's what you're looking at. Killing me won't change anything."

"Oh, I won't be killing only you. I'll blow up that entire truck and kill everyone on it—including your father."

Asher saw the moment Troy realized what Asher had meant when he said his father was coming to say goodbye. "Your father is going to die with you tonight, and there won't be a single thing you can do about it. Now you'll know how it feels to have the people you love ripped away from you," he said, his voice a deep growl.

"I already know. You can thank Alistair for that," Troy responded through gritted teeth.

Asher cocked his head. "What does Alistair have to do with this?" he asked, wondering what else his brother could possibly be hiding.

Troy scoffed. "You really know so little."

"I *knew* so little, but luckily for me I employed a very competent team. Soon I will know everything, and I will destroy every single person you've conspired against me with—and then, I'm going to take all seven kingdoms. The entire world will know Santina, and I have you to thank for that. I would've been content just to rule Santina, but not anymore. Now I will take kingdom after kingdom—starting with Adani."

Troy's jaw almost fell open and Asher smiled at his response. "You underestimated me, Troy, and you were the one who should've known what I'm capable of. That is your greatest failure."

Troy looked away but Asher didn't miss he was gritting his teeth.

Asher heard commotion behind him and realized the teams had arrived.

"Your father's here," Asher said, making sure Troy caught his smile before he turned and left, the guard locking the cell behind him.

ASHER

"Uncle," Asher said as he came face to face with the man he'd trusted—his father's brother. His uncle's eyes blazed and he looked defiant, not bothering to respond.

"Cuff him to a bed. I have something I want him to watch," Asher said.

His uncle's eyes narrowed and Asher raised an eyebrow.

"Did you really think you'd get away with it?" Asher asked.

The flash in his uncle's eyes indicated he had thought exactly that.

"Well, now you're going to pay," Asher continued. "You murdered two people I loved, two people whose lives were cut short because of your own selfish greed. Why did you do it?" he asked. "Was it the power? The money?"

"Neither," his uncle said, almost spitting on Asher. "I was righting the wrongs in this world."

Asher's eyebrows threaded together. "What wrongs?"

His uncle looked deep into his eyes. "Your father was unfit to rule. And you're the same. You're both too *weak*."

Anger blazed in Asher's chest. "Weak? My father was not *weak*!" Asher said through clenched teeth. "I'm going to show you something now, and then you can decide if you still think I'm weak."

Asher looked at James, who stood on the other side of the bed with a needle in his hand, and nodded. James inserted the needle into his uncle's vein—which was quite impressive given that his uncle was fighting against the restraints. Asher didn't want to think about how much experience James had doing this.

"Wheel him in. Make sure their beds face each other," Asher commanded as he continued to watch his uncle.

Asher heard the wheels of Troy's bed, but he knew the moment his uncle saw his son, because his composure cracked.

He turned his head, pleased to see Troy's IV was already underway.

"That's a morphine bag connected to his arm," Asher said, loud enough for them both to hear. "He's going to die the same way Noah died, so you know how I felt. You're going to watch him die—and then you'll die too."

"You're going to pay for this!" his uncle roared, his voice laced with panic.

"No," Asher replied coolly, "I'm going to be praised for executing the king's slayers." He raised an eyebrow, but his uncle's fury continued to burn in his eyes.

Asher put his hands on his uncle's head, ignoring his protests. Asher angled his head and said, "Watch."

His uncle continued to fight against the restraints but it was a futile attempt.

"Do you still think I'm weak?" Asher asked as he cradled his uncle's head.

When his uncle didn't respond, Asher screamed, "Do you still think I'm *weak*?"

"No, no!" his uncle began to yell. "No . . ." he continued, his voice trailing off as Troy became visibly sedated and the screen of his heart monitor confirmed he was beginning to fade.

"It hurts, doesn't it?" Asher said, his voice low and harsh. "It hurts to have the ones you love ripped away from you."

"No!" his uncle wailed again, but Asher forced him to look and James held a second scalpel ready to subdue him.

Asher watched as the dips in the line became smaller and smaller, and then Troy flatlined.

"No!"

"Now you can burn in hell!" Asher said bitterly before looking at James, fire burning in his eyes. "Finish it!"

He turned and walked out of the room before his composure cracked. His entire body was trembling and he felt sick to his stomach. He didn't feel remorse, but he felt . . . angry, hurt. It was such a waste—Troy could've done so much good in this world, but he'd chosen the wrong path.

"You okay?"

Asher recognized James's voice and he slowed his pace, allowing James to catch up to him in a few steps.

"I don't know," Asher admitted.

"Taking a life is hard, no matter whose it is. But they deserved to die, Asher. You have nothing to feel remorse or shame for. They chose their path and they were fully aware of the consequences," James said.

"I know," Asher said, looking ahead. "I'm going to my suite."

James walked beside him but didn't say another word. Security stood outside the suite, indicating Abi was inside.

They opened the door for Asher and closed it behind him. No one followed him in—James must've somehow indicated to his staff that Asher wasn't in the mood for company.

"Asher?" Abi asked as she walked toward the door. Her smile fell when she looked at him. "What's going on?"

Asher ran his palms over his face. "I don't know who I am anymore."

"Okay," Abi said gently, not reacting. She took his hand, leading him to the kitchen. "Sit for a minute," she said.

She searched through the kitchen until she found a bottle of wine. Asher focused on her, watching every little movement, using her as a distraction from the darkness lingering in his soul. He wondered if it had always been there, dormant, waiting for the opportunity to expose itself. Or was he transforming into someone he couldn't reconcile with the old Asher? He was scared he was losing himself. He'd changed so much in the last month; who would he be in a year?

Abi placed a glass of wine in front of him and sat beside him.

Asher took a mouthful as he tried to find the words to explain what had just happened. "They're dead," he said, failing to find more eloquent words.

She paused, and then her eyes widened. "Your Uncle and Troy," she said quietly. Asher didn't think she was surprised by what had happened but that he'd done it so quickly. His uncle had barely been in the palace five minutes.

"It was so different than I thought it was going to be," Asher admitted, bringing the glass back to his lips. "I thought I would feel . . . remorse, some guilt . . . but I felt justified . . . vindicated. My uncle called my father weak and said the same of me. Something inside me snapped." He shook his head. "Over the past few days I kept wondering if Troy had been led astray." Asher turned over his palms, pausing for a moment. "His behavior," he finally said, "is impossible for me to reconcile with the person I knew."

Abi squeezed his hands. "If your father had asked you to lead a revolt against the King of Santina, your own blood relative, would you have done it?" she asked.

Asher's eyebrows threaded together. "No," he said. "Of course not."

Abi gave a gentle, knowing smile. "Of course not. The truth we need to face is most often the ugliest truth," she said, almost whimsically. "The person you thought you knew wasn't real. Troy showed you a manufactured version of himself, one that he'd been grooming for many years. So don't grieve the manufactured version, because he never existed. The man who died today was a cold-blooded murderer."

"Yeah," Asher said, nodding. He rubbed his arms, suddenly feeling cold. "I don't know what to do now."

"Finish that glass of wine, have a hot shower, and get some sleep. We'll figure everything else out in the morning," Abi said, threading her fingers through his.

Asher brought them to his lips and kissed the knuckles of her fingers.

"I'm worried about where Grace is . . ." Asher said, his voice trailing off with his thoughts.

"Thomas Security will find her—it's their job to worry about that. Tomorrow, you can release the news about the executions, and the people of Santina will love you for it. They need closure for the death of their king, and who better to give it to them than their new king?"

Asher swallowed the last of his wine and sighed heavily. He looked at his hands, but the tremble had subsided. "Let's go to bed," he said, sounding drained even to his own ears.

ASHER STARED at the coffee machine as a trickle of coffee filled his mug. He'd assumed he'd have trouble sleeping last night, but he hadn't—he'd slept solidly all night and didn't know what to make of that—he could contribute it to sheer exhaustion, but if he was being honest, he would admit a large part of being able to sleep came down to the executions. He felt at peace with it—no remorse, no regret, no shame. And the more he thought about that, the more it troubled him.

He shook his head, forcing himself to concentrate on making his mug of coffee. When it was done, he carried it to his office. He sat at his father's desk and put his mug on a coaster that had been buried beneath stacks of mail. Asher ran his hands over the desk. His father was not weak, and he would not allow the people of Santina to think that.

Asher would protect his legacy.

A knock at the door dragged him from his thoughts. James entered.

"How did you sleep?" he asked, taking a seat opposite Asher.

"Surprisingly good," Asher said.

James eyed him, seeming to watch him carefully, then nodded. "Good. We need to talk about what happens next."

"What does happen next? How is the revolt dismantled?" Asher asked.

"Reed and his teams will stay behind for a few months to deal with this issue specifically. Samuel will monitor communications and we'll keep tabs on people. Groups like this usually go two ways: they either tend to lose hope and usually dismantle when their leaders are killed, so when you announce the executions tomorrow that should do most of the work. Or, they'll become martyrs and revenge their leader. We don't know how widespread this revolt is, so it's hard to say which way things will go."

Asher sighed. "Well, let's hope it's not the latter. But regardless, once the revolt is dismantled, what happens from there? Can Jesse's teams maintain security?"

"We'll make that call soon," James said, "but I seriously doubt it—Jesse needs more men than he has, and men without an interest in Santina would be ideal. Anyway, I have a hunch I'm going to get a request from one of my guys to remain here on the ground."

"What? Why?" Asher asked as he silently tried to guess who that might be.

"Just a hunch," James said with an odd smile. "Anyway, I just wanted to check in and make sure you're doing okay. Give me a call if you need anything."

"Thank you," Asher said again, and he really meant it. James Thomas had become a friend of sorts, and Asher had never made friends easily because of his royal status. Everyone had always wanted something from him, but he couldn't think of anything James could want . . . except a paycheck.

Asher grimaced at the bill that was coming—which reminded him to check his telephone messages.

He saw the light flashing on the telephone system and sure enough there was one from the King Khalil.

King Asher, we request an urgent meeting to discuss the contract of the Lithe Ruins and our oil wells. Please call me at your earliest convenience.

Asher scoffed at the politeness of his tone of voice and marveled at the nerve of the guy. *Lithe Ruins and* our *oil wells?*

They were *Santina's* oil wells, and Asher was not giving them up. Either the Adani king hadn't seen Asher's speech, or he was a fool for thinking Asher was bluffing because Asher was not handing over the Ruins.

Not at any cost.

ABI

Strong hands wrapped around her waist, drawing her in. She knew it was him from the touch of his hands, the smell of his cologne, and she sighed, dropping her head back to rest on his shoulder.

"What are you doing hiding in the gardens?" Asher asked. "You're a hard woman to find."

Abi chuckled. "Samuel couldn't locate my security team for you? I'd imagine I'm pretty easy to find these days."

She felt Asher's chest rumble as he gave a soft laugh. "I try not to ask him to do everything. At some point I'm going to have to run my life without speaking commands aloud in my office and things automatically turning on or occurring . . . that's going to be a sad day," he joked.

Abi turned in his arms. She saw security loitering nearby, but paid them no attention. She'd thought it would take a long time to get used to being constantly watched, especially when she was with Asher, but the teams were surprisingly good at making themselves feel invisible, and true to their word, they weren't actually watching Asher and Abi —they were watching everything happening around them.

"You didn't answer my question," Asher said as he kissed her forehead, his lips soft yet strong.

"What was the question?" Abi asked, struggling to think clearly.

Asher chuckled. "What are you doing out here?"

"Oh," Abi said, grinning. "Just thinking. I'm worried about the second part of that tape," she admitted.

"I'll take care of it," Asher said without hesitation.

"You can't say that when you don't know what you're dealing with," Abi said gently.

"My plan is to never find out. I've just released a statement to the media, releasing the names of the two people executed in relation to the murders, and that will show I'm a man who fulfils every promise I make. I've ensured that the people behind the tape are very aware of what will happen to them if they try to blackmail me," Asher said with a fierceness that made Abi look up and search his eyes.

"How do you feel today?" she asked, searching his eyes.

"Good," he admitted, like he himself was surprised by that admission. "Thank you for last night. I felt like I was spiraling . . . into a dark place. You were a voice of reason and I don't know how I would've handled last night without you." He looked into her eyes and there was a sadness in them. "I'm at peace with the executions because the people I thought they were never really existed, and that's the sad part. The fact that they are dead—two vindictive, conniving, murderers—isn't sad."

Abi tightened her grip on him, drawing him closer. "You've given all of Santina a gift, but especially your mother. She lost a son and her husband, and now you've given her justice for them."

Asher nodded, planting another kiss on her forehead. "I feel like I can breathe a little easier. And like there's two less people with guns pointed at my back."

Abi kissed his chest.

"Come with me," he said as he unwrapped her arms from his waist and took her hands, leading her inside. Security surrounded them, closer than usual.

"What's with the lack of personal space?" Abi asked under her breath.

Asher's lips turned up. "The news of the executions has broken, so they're going to be extra vigilant today, just in case there's any retaliation."

"How likely is that?" she asked Asher, then looked past him to Jesse.

"We don't know, it's just a precaution," Jesse said, seemingly at ease.

"Okay," Abi responded gratefully, and Asher gave her hand a squeeze as they walked back to the palace.

The sun had fallen long ago and the palace was lit up. Abi didn't think it had ever looked more beautiful. In that moment she fully realized for the first time she that she would never return to her apartment. She'd known that, of course, but the reality was just hitting her.

The palace was her home now. Her home with Asher.

She looked up past the tall stone walls of the palace to a sky littered with shining stars. The night sky reminded her of her first date with Asher at the Ruins, and marveled at how that seemed like a lifetime ago. So much had happened in such a short time, but with the murderers now dead, Abi prayed the coming weeks would bring a new fate for Santina.

***

"How is my favorite daughter?" William Bennett asked.

Abi's eyes snapped up, leaving her computer for the first time all morning.

"You do realize that all your children are aware you call each of them your favorite, right?" she asked with a sweet smile.

Her father grinned. "But I really like you the most," he joked. "How is Asher today?"

"He's okay . . ." Abi said, looking up as the door opened and Asher walked in. "You can ask him yourself."

William turned and stood with an extended hand. "I was just

asking Abi how you are. I can't imagine yesterday was easy for you, even if it was the right thing to do."

"I'm okay," Asher said. "I'm processing it, and probably will be for some time, but I don't feel remorse for their deaths."

William nodded then gave a sad smile. "You remind me so much of your father; it's like I'm standing here with him thirty years ago."

Asher smiled. "How would you have described him?"

William lifted an eyebrow and seemed to think it through. "Brave, kind, resilient . . . stubborn," he said with a twinkle in his eye, then added, "A natural-born leader who got better with age, that's how I'd describe him. He made hard decisions—decisions I'd never envied—and it takes a strong person to be able to do that."

Asher nodded, the smile slowly fading from his face.

"But I'm not here to talk about your father. I did want to check in on you . . . and then talk business," William said.

Abi gave a barely audible groan. William didn't miss it—but he did ignore it.

"I've been waiting for the right time to sit down with you. Today hardly seems like it, but never does any other day. And maybe you need a distraction now more than ever. So, I've made a few notes I'd like you to look over and then we can discuss them. I know business, Asher, but you know politics, so these are just notes," he said, passing Asher a notebook. "Santina needs money to thrive, and if you can secure international funding within the next six months—combined with the executions—you'll have the highest ratings of any king Santina has ever seen."

Asher nodded. "Leave it with me. I'll review it over the next two days and get back to you." His eyes dropped to the notebook as turned page after page of handwritten notes. "On further thought, give me a week and I'll get back to you."

William beamed a smile. "Sounds like a good plan," he said with a nod. He turned to leave, but then looked over his shoulder. "Asher, if you need anything, please call me. You're family now, and I will do anything for my family." He turned to Abi. "You should call me more often too," he said with a smile before walking out.

Abi looked to Asher, almost surprised. "My father is not normally so . . . warm. You're the son he never had. Call him if you need anything—he truly means that. I know he's not a replacement for your father, but he'll be there for you."

"I will. I appreciate that." Asher sat opposite her, and Abi noted they'd switched roles—she was the one behind the desk.

Abi tilted her head for a moment. "If our firstborn was a girl, would you let her lead?" she asked suddenly.

"Yes," he said without pause. "In fact, if we have a daughter who is anything like you, I might let her lead regardless of any older siblings," he said with the first real smile she'd seen him wear in a while. "And that's a decision we would make together." Asher's gaze swept over the office. "It looks good."

"Alistair gave me this painting," Abi said, turning to look at the wall behind her.

"Alistair?" Asher asked with wide eyes. "I've seen this painting before . . ."

Abi grinned. "It's by a local artist, and it was a big exhibition piece six months ago. Apparently Alistair went on a binge and decided it was a good buy."

"Alistair is full of surprises at the moment," he said with a smile, leaning over her desk. He placed a finger under her chin, tilting her lips to his. "Have dinner with me tonight."

"Sure," she said. "Where?" Abi couldn't imagine Asher wanting to go out for dinner, but that didn't mean there weren't options.

"The gardens," he said, his eyes locking on hers. "I have to go—I have an important meeting—but I'll see you in a few hours."

She closed her eyes as he kissed her goodbye. She couldn't say she loved the idea of any execution, but Asher had been different since last night. Calmer, more at peace, and more attentive to her. It wasn't that he'd necessarily said or done anything different, but the way he looked at her had changed. It had brought them closer together, and she knew if they could handle the pressures they were under right now, they could make it regardless of what life threw at them in the future.

ASHER

Asher kissed her forehead, inhaling the scent of her perfume. "I'll see you in a few hours," he said, before turning to leave.

James was waiting outside the door for Asher.

"Is he here?" Asher asked.

James nodded. "He's waiting in the sitting room."

Asher walked in that direction, both excited and a little nervous for what he was about to do—not because he was unsure of his decision, but because this was something Abi would wear for the rest of her life, and he wanted her to love it.

"Mr. Golding, thank you for coming on such short notice," Asher said, extending his hand.

The Royal Jeweler stood, his handshake firm and confident. "For you, Your Majesty, anything."

Asher simply nodded. "Please come with me," he said as James Thomas lingered close, like a shadow.

Asher took Mr. Golding to his office and motioned for him to sit.

Mr. Golding opened his bag, laid out some velvet trays, and put on a pair of white gloves.

"I have something special I want to show you. This piece only came to me yesterday—it's interesting how things work out, isn't it? I almost wasn't going to buy it, but . . . call it intuition . . . I decided to." Mr. Golding opened the velvet box and Asher's jaw fell open.

"Wow," Asher whispered.

"Eighteen carats, emerald-cut on a platinum band. A simple yet breathtaking design," he said, placing the ring on the velvet tray.

Asher stared at it. "That's . . . huge," he said, lost for a more eloquent word.

"It's beautiful," James Thomas said, leaning in.

Asher bit his lip, looking up. He didn't expect James to have an opinion.

"You like it?" Asher asked.

James chuckled. "Well, not for me. But for Abi, sure. That's a spectacular diamond."

"How much do you know about diamonds?" Asher asked, genuinely interested.

"Not that much except for the research I did before buying Mak's," he said, still looking at the ring.

"How much is it?" Asher asked Mr. Golding, who seemed particularly pleased with the direction of this conversation.

"For you, a deal," he said with a sparkle in his eyes. "The budget you gave me—it's right at the top. Not a dollar more," he said, clasping his hands on the table.

Asher almost laughed at the way he seemed pleased with himself for coming in on budget, even if it was a larger-than-usual budget. "I'll take it," Asher said.

James nodded his approval.

Mr. Golding picked up the ring, put it a box, and pressed it into Asher's hand. "Congratulations, Your Majesty."

"Thank you," Asher said. "Regarding payment—"

Mr. Golding shook his head. "None is required. Your mother recently donated some items we auctioned off, raising over half a billion dollars for a local charity. This ring is our gift of appreciation."

Asher all but picked his jaw up off the floor. "When did she do this?" He hadn't been aware of any such auction.

Mr. Golding gave a sad smile. "About a week before your father's death. She said she hated for them to sit in the drawer unused. So, we auctioned them off for her, and any stone that has belonged to a royal family is worth ten times the retail value of the actual stone. We donated the proceeds to her charity of choice: one for orphaned children. The auction was kept silent, out of respect for your family and the buyers. They are typically very wealthy and private people who do not want their names in the papers."

"I don't know what to say other than thank you," Asher said simply.

"It is my pleasure. I am certain it will be the correct size given the measurements you provided, but please do let me know if any adjustments need to be made."

"Of course," Asher said, feeling nervous carrying such an expensive item. How was Abi going to feel with it on her finger?

"And as per your friend's request," Mr. Golding said, shooting James a look. "This is the replica ring that she can wear when there are security concerns."

Asher's eyebrows lifted. He took the ring, studying it. He opened the box and placed them side by side. He could barely tell the difference. "This isn't a diamond?"

Mr. Golding chuckled. "Amazing, isn't it? I had a customer bring her ring in to sell after a bitter divorce. It became even more bitter when she realized the ring she'd been wearing all those years was a fake. That man may contact you in need of your services," he said to James with a small laugh.

James grinned. "He'd better start running now."

Mr. Golding continued to chuckle while he picked up his bag. Asher put the fake ring aside, careful not to mix them up. Then he tucked the box into his jacket pocket.

James escorted Mr. Golding out while Asher reviewed the new stack of mail on his desk—it was never ending. He'd barely managed to sort through half of it before James returned, taking a seat opposite him.

"Media is good this morning," James commented.

Asher nodded. "I read some of it. Any sighting of Aunty?"

"No," James admitted. "We think she's gone underground—into hiding. We have alerts set up for her on multiple systems, including voice and face recognition systems. We're also backtracking her activities for the last twelve months. She had help escaping her home and I think someone is still helping her hide now—which indicates she's involved in the revolt, we just don't know to what degree. I think she'll try and get out of Santina completely. That would be her best move."

Asher nodded. "How are you backtracking her movements?"

"Telephone calls, appointments made online and appointments noted in the paper diary we found in her home, facial recognition matches. Anything we can. Samuel and his team are working on this full time."

"Good. Any other news?" Asher asked.

"Not regarding the revolt or Abi's tape. Most of the chatter is about the executions, which is exactly what we want."

"I responded to the voicemail today," Asher said with another nod. "I advised the king there would be no meeting to discuss the Lithe Ruins and *my* oil wells."

"Good," James responded. "The teams there have completed the additional testing this morning, and there's twice as much oil as was estimated in the sale contract. I'm not sure what that means . . . probably that Troy was trying to screw Alistair on the deal so his friends could pay half the price they should've if it was a legitimate deal."

"I am not handing over this land. It is part of Santina, and I will not sell it," Asher said, adamant.

"I wouldn't either," James said. "But you will need to be prepared for some kind of fallout over this. Adani wants this land, or more correctly, they want a piece of your pie. This is probably more of a political statement than it is about the oil."

"I agree," Asher said, "and I'll deal with that soon. I need to review William Bennett's notebook of plans and confirm a strategy, because the stronger my international relationships are, the less of a problem Adani will be."

James nodded but there was hesitation in his eyes.

"What?" Asher asked.

James sighed. "Almost certainly, Adani has the tape of Abi—or a copy at least. I suspect they'll release the tape in its entirety within the next few days."

"And I'll punish them for that by releasing details of how they poisoned their poor," Asher said, raising an eyebrow.

"So then we need to be prepared for any form of backlash," James said. "I'll leave you to it. Enjoy your dinner," he finished with a grin.

ASHER

Asher walked around the table his mother had taken upon herself to decorate. She was appalled at Asher's first proposal and had done her best to ensure this one would impress her future daughter-in-law. A tall vase overflowed with cascading flowers and the surrounding trees were lit up with fairy lights. Every detail was immaculate and intimate and perfect. Asher owed his mother for this one, but he also thought it had been a good distraction for her this afternoon.

He put a hand on his chest, feeling the box tucked inside—making sure the ring was still there.

"They're here," Jesse said, tapping his shoulder. "We'll be nearby."

"Thanks, Jesse," Asher said as Abi walked into view.

She came to a stop, her jaw dropping open as he held out his hand.

"What is this?" she asked with a beaming smile.

"Dinner," Asher said with a wink. He cupped her cheeks and brushed his lips over hers. The kiss sent a shiver through him.

"This is . . . I have no words," she said, putting a hand on her chest.

Asher chuckled. He tugged her hands and she fell forward but he caught her. "I've got you," he said, and he meant every word.

Abi straightened and wrapped her arms around his neck. "And I've got you," she said as he pressed his lips to hers again.

She deepened the kiss but he pulled back before he cancelled dinner altogether.

"Have a seat," he said, pulling out a chair for her.

He sat beside her, wanting to be close. His parents had always sat side by side, rather than across from each other, even when it was only the two of them dining. Asher had never thought much about that until now.

"Who organized this?" Abi asked. "It's amazing." She suddenly turned to him. "Are we getting married tonight?"

Asher laughed heartily. "No. My mother asked me how I proposed and she was most disappointed. She told me it was completely unsatisfactory and I must do it again, better this time. So, clearly she didn't have a lot of faith in me, and here we are. She organized this table today—this afternoon."

"I owe her a thank you," Abi said, looking over the table.

Asher stood, reaching for the bottle of champagne.

"Vintage Dom. Oh, we are celebrating tonight!" Abi said in appreciation.

"I found this in the cellar," Asher admitted. "I think it must've been a gift because my mother doesn't drink a lot of champagne. And it's the one thing Alistair didn't drink."

"Well, thank you to whoever bought us this very nice bottle," Abi said, clinking her glass.

Asher stretched out his legs and took a sip of his champagne. "Not bad," he said, taking her hand and threading their fingers together.

"What did you do this afternoon?" Abi asked.

"I looked over your father's notes," Asher said with wide eyes. "He has detailed quite the plan. I'm busy groveling for money over the next few months," he joked, but it wasn't far from the truth.

Abi whistled. "He is relentless," she admitted with a strained laugh, then looked into his eyes. "Santina is lucky to have you," she said more quietly.

He smiled sadly. "I just want them to be proud—proud to be a

Santinian. We were once regarded as the greatest kingdom in the region."

"Many still think that, Asher. Santina has always been highly respected because we stand up for what we believe in. Sure, there's been a few corruption issues and a few traitors, but Santina and our people have always rallied. And although we may not be as wealthy as our neighbors, we are proof that money doesn't solve all problems. Actually, if you have weaknesses, money will amplify them. Adani is proof of that."

"And yet they've gotten away with it for so long," Asher said bitterly.

"Perhaps their luck has run out," she said, looking into Asher's eyes.

He nodded. "We'll see what cards they play."

"Anyway, let's talk about that another day," she said, her voice suddenly bubbly and light. "Let's talk about something fun."

"Fun?" Asher asked with an amused laugh. He couldn't remember the last time he'd done something fun. "Like what?"

"Like when are we going to get married?" Abi asked, leaning in to kiss him.

"Tomorrow," Asher answered without hesitation.

Abi laughed. "I hope your mother can plan a wedding in five minutes, then."

"Oh she could, I'm sure. I don't think she thought this day would ever come," Asher mused.

"No, I don't think she did," Abi said with a smile. "Neither did Santina, I'm sure."

"There's hope for everyone yet," Asher joked. "Seriously, though, when do you want to get married?"

"As soon as we can," Abi said. "Let's set a date by the end of the week."

"Deal," Asher said happily.

Abi paused for a second, biting her lip. "Let's play a game," she said suddenly, her voice a notch higher.

Asher gave her a wary look. "What kind of game?"

"A fun one," she said, laughing. "We would often play it when on IFRT business . . . when there was a lot of downtime sitting around waiting for things to happen. This is how it works: I'll ask you a question and you have to answer it immediately. You can't think about it—just say the first thing that pops into your mind."

Asher eyed her. "This could be dangerous."

"I'll ask good questions. Do you trust me?" she asked.

"Yes," he responded immediately. "Was that the start of the game?"

Abi laughed. "No, first question: an easy one . . . what's your favorite food?"

"Italian. Pizza," Asher said.

"Dream job," Abi said.

"Being Mr. Abigail Bennett," he said with a smirk.

She scoffed. "Flattery will get you far," she said, then looked thoughtful for a moment. "Favorite thing about me?'

"You're brave," he said without hesitation.

"Hmm," she said. "I'll take that. What did you love most about your father?"

"He stayed true to his values," Asher said.

"And what did you love most about Noah?"

"He was funny—especially as a kid. It's sad that we lose our humor as we grow older," Asher mused, then smiled. "Now it's my turn."

"Okay," Abi said with daring eyes.

"Favorite thing to do on the weekends?"

"Sleep," she said, and then added, "and watch home-renovation shows."

"Do you want to renovate a home?" Asher asked.

"No," Abi said, chuckling. "I just like watching others do it."

"That's weird, but okay," Asher said, grinning. "What is your dream holiday destination?"

"Maldives."

"How many children do you want?"

"Three," she said, raising an eyebrow.

"Boys or girls?" he asked.

"Healthy," she fired back.

"When did you know you loved me?" Asher asked, watching her carefully.

She took a moment to think about it. "A few weeks after our date at the Ruins . . . when I knew I was going to lose you and I couldn't bear the thought."

Asher cupped her cheeks and kissed her deeply. "You never lost me," he whispered, his voice thick.

He pushed his chair back and got down on one knee. "Marry me, Abi. I don't want to live a day without you. I want to wake up to you every morning, I want you to bear my *three* children," he said with a smile. "I want us to have our own family and I want to know that no matter what is wrong in the world, we will always have each other."

"Yes. That's the easiest question of my life," she said with wet eyes.

Asher pulled the box from his jacket and opened it.

Abi gasped. "Holy shit," she said, then giggled. "Well, that was elegant."

Asher chuckled as he took the ring from the box and slid it onto her finger. As Mr. Golding had said it would be, it was a perfect fit.

Abi wiggled her fingers. "I'm speechless, yet again. You have to stop doing this to me. I'm normally much wittier, but I can't think past this ring."

"Good. That's the perfect response," Asher said, bringing her hand to his lips. "You're my queen," he said. "And I don't just mean the title. Everything now is about us. I will always look after you, and I will always trust you and respect you. We're partners and equals in this crazy life we'll live."

Abi nodded as a tear ran down her cheek. She wiped it away quickly, as if she were embarrassed. "I don't know who I am right now," she said quietly.

"A happy woman, I hope," Asher said, playfully.

Abi beamed a smile. "More than you'll ever know." And with that, she pressed her lips to his and he lost himself in the kiss, in every sensation of the woman who would be his wife.

REED

Reed spun on his heels, his weapon raised. His eyes scanned the white walls, checking for movement behind the arches. He exhaled slowly, his finger steady on the trigger.

He heard no movement and saw no movement.

But something wasn't right.

He'd felt uneasy all afternoon even though the palace had been quiet.

Reed retreated the way he'd just come. He moved in closer to the building, letting his shoulder rub on the old stone palace walls. A gust of hot wind blew through the loggia; he had come to love the warm Santina breeze that lingered long after the sun fell.

The breeze calmed him a little now, and he felt a little less like something was off, but he'd learned to trust his instincts.

Reed walked slowly, his footsteps silent and careful.

"Samuel, check the cameras in the south garden," Reed whispered under his breath. "Check the last fifteen minutes."

"*Copy*," Samuel said. He didn't ask any questions, didn't question Reed.

Reed continued to creep forward. He was doing his second check of the grounds, despite having done one less than ten minutes ago and having security teams stationed along the perimeter walls.

Reed looked to the walls and spotted his men. "Perimeter guards, check in," Reed said.

He held his breath as the men responded one by one. When all thirty-five of them responded, he felt his shoulders drop a little.

"No movement except the rustling of trees," Samuel responded.

"Thanks," Reed said, but he didn't let down his guard.

Maybe it was all in his mind, maybe he was tired and it was the relentless pressure of a job where mistakes could be fatal.

Reed could make those arguments in his head, but he didn't believe them—not for a second.

He crept forward, pausing at the corner of the tower, then stood so still he could've been mistaken for a statue. He barely dared to breathe as he took a moment to let himself feel . . . what, he didn't know.

His heart beat steady in his chest and he used the rhythm of the beat to roughly count the seconds. A few minutes later, he was still standing there. His mind told him to go, but his legs refused to move.

"Jesse, check in," Reed said.

"Copy," Jesse responded immediately.

"Are you with Asher? Where's Abi?"

"I'm with Asher. Abi is in the tunnels," Jesse said.

Reed supposed he shouldn't have been surprised. They'd been monitoring her recent Google searches.

"Okay, good. Stay close to Asher," Reed said.

"What's wrong?" Jesse asked quickly.

Reed sighed. "Nothing, I just feel uneasy. I can't explain it," he said.

"Copy. Keep me updated," Jesse said, and Reed was grateful he hadn't needed to explain further. As much as they'd needed to investigate Jesse, his willingness to do anything they'd ever asked was the one thing that had always indicated his innocence. He wasn't after power, and he wasn't interested in leading them in a certain direction. Jesse was willing to do whatever needed to be done.

"Hey . . . I'm not sure . . ."

Reed's eyebrows threaded together as he strained to listen to the conversation Jesse had started with someone else.

Another gust of wind blew through, hitting the sweat on the back of his neck, cooling his body. He no longer cared about the stickiness of the dust that covered his skin when the warm winds blew; surprisingly, he'd come to love desert life in Santina.

"Alistair's up . . . two teams behind him," Jesse said under his breath.

"Copy," Reed said with a nod, realizing that he must've been speaking to Alistair or his team.

Reed's head snapped to the left at the sound of a stick breaking. He looked to the fruit orchard and bent down, sitting on his heels as he looked underneath the trees for movement.

"Samuel, fly a drone over the orchard. There's movement in there," Reed said, without a doubt in his mind.

"Copy," Samuel responded.

Reed's eyes scanned back and forth, scoping every tree trunk. They had every perimeter secure and set up with trip wires, and the tunnel entrances were manned and tripped with explosives if anyone entered from the outside.

The palace had been in lockdown since Asher had threatened the Adani king a few hours ago. Reed wished he could've seen the king's face when Asher had told him he had proof of their involvement in poisoning the water supply of their poor and if the full tape of Abi was released, Asher would personally hold the king responsible. The tape was recorded on Adani land, after all.

Reed was turning away when he noticed something on the ground by the arch. He looked over his shoulder, checking behind him.

"Orchard is clear," Samuel said.

"Copy," Reed responded, but his mind was on the dusting of a footprint a few meters in front of him. He crept forward and put his foot beside the barely visible print, confirming his suspicions. This footprint didn't belong to any of his men—it was far too small. It could've belonged to a servant, but they should've been locked down inside for the last few hours. And this print was definitely fresh, because it hadn't been swept away by the hot Santina breeze.

Reed pulled his phone out and sent Samuel a photo. "Look at the security surveillance for this area—my current location—for the past twelve hours," he said as his eyes darted up. There was no direct camera pointing at this position, but hopefully they'd get lucky.

He swept the back of his palm across his slick forehead. He needed a drink and he needed to get out of this thick heat.

But his eyes returned to the lone footprint. The ground didn't look like it had been cleaned, so how had only one footprint been created? Reed's head tilted back before he'd finished thinking that through.

And then he saw it. Another partial print on the column.

There weren't any prints on the ground because someone had climbed up the arch.

His blood turned cold. The palace had been in lockdown, but someone had already made their way inside, and now they'd locked them in.

He was still processing that realization when a thunderous roar rolled through the air as the palace shook.

"Jesse! Check in!" Reed screamed as he started sprinting for the tunnels.

But what he heard next chilled his blood.

"Jesse's dead," an unfamiliar voice said.

"Samuel! Code 23!" Reed commanded as his lungs fought to breathe through the shock as he skidded around the corner, changing direction and sprinting toward Asher's office.

They'd been infiltrated, and now someone had Jesse's communication device. Samuel would change them to a different frequency—except for Jesse's earpiece—and eliminate that problem. But Reed feared the worst: If someone had Jesse's earpiece, he was almost certainly dead as the voice had said—or at least so incapacitated that he couldn't fight back. The earpieces were small and hard to get in and out of the ear. It took time, and time wasn't something an intruder had when their target was fighting back.

Jesse was down. And that meant that Asher's team might be too.

"Team Delta, check in!" Reed shouted as he came hurtling around the corner so fast he almost slipped on the fine layer of dust that always settled on the loggia tiles regardless of it being cleaned every day.

He caught himself and sprinted forward and toward Asher.

ASHER

Two gunshots echoed through his office as the ground beneath him shook, and the guards inside Asher's office fell to their knees as their eyes rolled back. Asher's heart was in his throat and it took him a minute to see the holes in the drywall—the guards had been shot from outside.

The door flew open and a masked man strode in, aiming his weapon.

Asher looked down the barrel, paralyzed.

He couldn't breathe, he couldn't think. He wasn't trained for this.

Asher heard the click of the weapon—he couldn't say what part of the gun it was, but he'd watched enough movies to know that sound came a few seconds before the bullet.

His body felt cold and time seemed to pause. His life seemed to flash before him, but the sound of another gunshot brought him back to reality.

The masked man swayed then fell to his knees. James Thomas appeared behind him with a pistol pointed. His eyes swept over the office like two darts, pausing on his fallen men.

"The palace is under siege," James said quickly. "Let's go!"

"Where's Abi?" Asher asked as the reality of the situation struck him like hail in a thunderstorm.

"She's in the tunnels. She has a team and Reed's heading there now. But we need to move," James said, looking over his shoulder and then back to the window.

"And my mother and Alistair?"

"With their teams," James said, looking over his shoulder once more.

The glass windows shattered and James dove for cover behind Asher's desk, bringing him to the ground.

James looked to him, his dark eyes swirling with a fierceness Asher had never seen. "I'm getting you out of here, but I need you to listen to every word I say. We don't have time for you to question me."

Asher nodded rapidly, his stomach still in his throat.

"Stay here," James said as he crawled around the desk, toward the window. He sat back on his heels, using the wall for protection and raised his weapon. He seemed in no rush and was impossibly calm despite the urgency in his voice a few moments ago.

He fired six shots, then sprang to his feet and pulled the curtains shut before running back to Asher. "Help me move this desk," he said.

Asher jumped to his feet as they dragged his father's solid wood desk into the corner of the room.

Objects fell and mountains of paperwork slid into one another. Asher knew it didn't matter, but the thought that it was going to take him hours to sort out come anyway.

If you survive.

Asher shook his head.

He would survive—and he would make sure Abi and his family did too.

James tilted his head back and Asher realized he was looking at the trap door above.

"We need to go into the ceiling. There are men everywhere and I don't want to move you through the hallways," James said as he leaned down and dragged an arm across Asher's desk, pushing everything onto the floor.

"Come on!" James said, springing up onto the desk.

Asher climbed up as James pushed the trap door cover aside and motioned for Asher to go first.

Asher had no idea how to haul himself up into it, but he'd seen James do it on surveillance and tried to mimic the action. He grunted as he pushed up, pulling his knees to his chest. It took his eyes a few seconds to adjust to the maze of beams and insulation that surrounded him. He crawled forward, careful to keep his balance.

James was a second behind him and passed him an earpiece.

"Samuel, we're in," James said.

Gunfire sounded below them and Asher's breath caught in his throat. He quickly pushed the earpiece in.

"Head north until I tell you to stop," Samuel said.

Asher paused, realizing he had no idea which way was north, but James didn't have the same problem and surged ahead, Asher following without hesitation.

The thick dust settled in his lungs and he suppressed a cough.

"Keep moving," James urged.

Asher cleared his throat and focused on putting one hand and knee in front of the other, but he almost lost his balance when gunfire erupted and his head snapped up.

"It's underneath us—it's my men clearing the path for us and making sure no bullets are fired at the ceiling," James said quickly.

Asher continued on, struggling to keep up with James who crawled forward with an ease that Asher didn't feel.

"Where are we going?" Asher asked.

"To the garage," James said. "I'm going to get you out of the palace. I have two teams making their way there now. They'll escort you to the Bennetts' house, and I'll stay here and help the remaining teams."

"Where's Jesse? He was just outside my office," Asher said in a rush.

James didn't answer straight away and Asher's stomach churned, but he didn't have time to focus on it because gunfire erupted, breaking through the ceiling to their left.

James sprung to his feet. "Come on!"

Asher stood, careful to keep his balance. James grabbed his arm, guiding him across the beams, moving faster with each step. Asher's heart pounded in his chest and more than once he was thought he was going to lose his balance and fall through the ceiling.

All the while the gunfire continued to come, tracking them.

"How do they know we're in here?" Asher asked, breathless.

"They must be using thermal imaging," James said, skidding to a halt. He stopped at a box, flipping the lid off and pulling out two pistols and a selection of items that Asher thought included grenades—but he couldn't be sure.

It dawned on him then that Thomas Security must've positioned the boxes in the ceiling some time ago, in preparation for such an event.

"Let's go!" James said, running again.

Asher followed him, ignoring his burning lungs but grateful for the high ceilings that meant he could run upright for the most part.

"Drop through the next trap door," Samuel instructed as bullets fired through the ceiling, closer this time.

Neither man hesitated.

ABI

Abi blinked, her eyes blinded by the explosion. But when she opened her eyes, she couldn't see anything but darkness. She couldn't work out if she'd been temporarily blinded or if the power had been cut.

But she could hear, and the sounds she heard chilled her blood: gunshots, fighting, and the thud of punches landing and the cracking of bones breaking.

An arm grabbed her, spinning her around, and a scream roared from her throat. She fought back, every self-defense instinct kicking in. She had no idea what was going on, but she knew one thing for sure: she would not be taken again.

"Abi!" She heard the security guards calling her name and she yelled in response to them, and then second-guessed herself. Maybe it was better if no one could see her.

But with every moment that passed, her eyes adjusted and she fully realized the nightmare she was in.

There were so many men in the tunnel she could barely believe it. Where had they all come from?

The comprehension and questions were like flashes of lightning in her mind and then she flipped back into survival mode. There was no time to think, no time to ponder, only time to fight—because her life depended on it.

A body flew into her from behind, knocking her to the floor and the wind from her lungs. She pressed her palms into the ground when a gunshot rang through the air and the body above her jerked in response. She shivered and stayed deadly still, keeping her breathing calm and low. Could they see her? Right now, her best protection might be underneath the person she was sure wasn't breathing. The thought disturbed her, but her survival instinct was more powerful. She stayed underneath the body.

"Abi!" She recognized the voice this time: Rachel.

She stood by her head, swooped down, grabbed her hand and pulled her up. "Are you okay?" she asked, wiping something wet from her forehead.

"I think so," she said, her hand immediately tracing Rachel's. Her fingers caught the edge of her hair and she realized it was slick and coated in a warm, thick substance.

The realization hit her like a freight train; she didn't need to look at the body she'd rolled off her. He'd taken one in the chest and one in the head, and she was coated in his blood and likely some brain matter that Abi couldn't think about right now.

Rachel shoved a weapon in her hand. "Come on!"

Abi nodded as she moved the pistol into position, resting her finger on the trigger. She thought about the weapon James Thomas had given her and realized it was sitting on the chair a few meters away from where she stood. He'd warned her to keep it on her at all times, and the one minute she didn't have it, she'd been thrust into hell.

Movement behind Rachel drew her attention, and Abi raised her weapon and fired at the man with his weapon aimed at her friend's back. Rachel jolted at the sound of the gun and swung around, raising her own weapon. Abi spun around, back up against Rachel. She squinted to see, and to make sense of the chaos that surrounded them.

She needed to think clearly if they were going to survive.

Abi turned back around to see a figure coming at Rachel fast, but she ducked low and fired, landing one in his stomach.

"I was on my way to see you! What the hell is going on?" Rachel asked, breathless as she fired two more shots.

"I don't know but we need to get out of here! We need to stay together—"

Abi was cut off as an elbow slammed into the back of her head. She stumbled, falling forward, but Rachel grabbed her. Abi managed not to fall and instead swung around, raising her weapon, but no one was after her: she'd just been caught in the middle of two men fighting. It was just another reason they had to get out of there—there were too many bullets flying and if they weren't careful, they'd get shot.

"Run!" Abi grabbed Rachel, guiding her toward the exit that she knew was ahead. She took one look over her shoulder, seeing the Thomas Security men—the ones still standing—forming a protective barrier around them.

But Abi skidded to a halt and Rachel ran straight into the back of her.

Abi's heart thundered in her chest as she looked down the barrel of the woman's pistol.

"Don't move," the woman said, her voice like ice.

Who was she? She looked vaguely familiar, but Abi couldn't place her.

"Asher took my husband and my child, and now I'm going to take everything he loves," she said, her voice void of emotion. She sounded like she'd rehearsed this moment, prepared for it a thousand times.

Abi's mind spiraled as she processed what the woman had just said. The woman was Troy's mother, Grace.

How did she get into the tunnels? Thomas Security had been looking for her. Abi's attention was on the pistol in Grace's hand, but she didn't miss the device being held in her other hand. She couldn't be sure, but it looked like a detonator.

"Abi," a woman with a slightly shaky voice said from behind Grace.

Abi's breath caught in her throat as she recognized the voice.

Emilia. Abi squinted, straining to see. It was too dark, but even still she could see a figure beside Emilia and Abi knew by the angle of the person's hand a pistol was pointed at Emilia's head.

"You're making a huge mistake," Abi said, returning her attention to the woman in front of her.

The corner of the woman's lips turned up. "No, they made a huge mistake assuming Martin Snider was a man. They thought he was my husband and he'd influenced my son, didn't they?" she asked coldly. "Maybe they thought I was involved, but did they ever once really consider that I might be Martin Snider?"

"Grace!" Emilia gasped.

Grace gave a chilling smile, her eyes not leaving Abi's. "No one saw it coming. And that was why it was so perfect. My husband and my son were the front, because the soldiers would never have allied with me. But I was behind it all. Every plan. Every murder. And I planned the perfect distraction today: I set up an attack that would focus all your guards on Asher, leaving everyone else at risk. I knew you were down here," she said, her eyes hauntingly cold. "I have friends in the palace."

Abi saw Emilia step forward, her face tight and ashen.

"Do not move!" Abi commanded, speaking directly to Grace, but she was really speaking to Emilia.

Grace's eyes didn't leave Abi, and her confident expression didn't falter.

"What did we do to your family?" Emilia demanded. "What did we do to deserve this?"

"You and your husband were useless," Grace replied coolly. "And then, to make it worse, you were going to hand the throne over to your privileged son. Santina's fate rested in the hands of a young man who'd never been groomed for the role of king. It should've been us. We would have *saved* Santina!" she said, a slight tremble entering her voice. Grace was beginning to unravel but Abi wasn't sure that was a good thing. What would happen when she took her finger off that device in her hand? "And then Alistair did the same thing to Troy when he stole his girlfriend and knocked her up. Your family is ignorant and careless. You would've ruined Santina. You had to be stopped for the greater good of us all."

"What do you want?" Abi asked, trying to stall her so that she could formulate a plan. Men were still fighting in the tunnel, and the rest of the guards were likely with Asher. Abi had to figure this out on her own. "Your husband and son are dead."

"You still don't get it, do you? I wanted my husband and son to lead with me, but now I'll do it alone. So, I want you all to die. Santina deserves better!" Grace said, raising her voice. Abi wondered why Grace hadn't considered Alistair a threat to the throne—and it was only then that Abi realized there was another figure beside Emilia.

Abi felt the wind knock from her lungs yet again. Alistair was beside her! Abi, Emilia and Alistair were all in the tunnels—everyone Asher loved.

"That doesn't help you," Abi continued. She had to keep Grace talking, had to stall. "Alistair has a son who would become the next heir when he comes of age. You will never rule Santina!"

"I will if I'm the last living relative. And I will kill them all. Everyone—including the child," she said with an arrogance that disturbed Abi. Why was she so confident?

"Who do you think is backing you right now? Adani?" Abi asked. "When Asher learns of this, Adani will be destroyed before sunrise. With the information he has about them poisoning their poor, they won't survive. Asher won't even have to send in his army—the Adani people will be so incensed they'll destroy the royal family themselves."

Grace smiled. "Adani is helpful, but I will do this without them. How do you think I got in here with my men? It seems not everyone—your staff members included—think Asher is fit to rule. I had help getting in here, and I will have help taking the throne. Everything is in place. It can't be stopped."

"Of course it can be stopped," Abi said quickly. "A new deal can always be made."

Abi didn't think Asher was going to be in the mood for negotiating with Grace but every second mattered now. Every second Abi could stall Grace was another second they were alive and able to escape.

"I don't want to make a new deal. I want them all to die," she said without a hint of remorse.

"That's not going to happen. You should use me to negotiate for you," Abi said. She knew she was baiting her, but she had zero options right now.

Grace stood still, as if thinking about it.

And then she lifted her finger off the device.

ABI

*A*bi's ears rang as the ground beneath her feet shook. She lost her balance, almost stumbling, but she managed to keep upright and keep her eyes on Grace.

But her relief was short-lived as another thunderous roar was followed by the sound of a sickening crack.

The lights in the tunnel flickered, but stayed on—had Samuel done that? Suddenly Abi felt less alone, but the lighting brought on a new shiver of dread as she looked over the bloody bodies on the floor of the tunnel. How many were Thomas Security guys? At least ten of them had to be. Another six men were in a standoff farther down the tunnel, and two men stood by Emilia and Alistair, weapons pointed at them—definitely not Thomas Security men.

Abi's eyes swept over the entire scene. In a normal situation, she would just shoot Grace, but she was wielding a weapon that none of them knew the potential of. Could she blow up the entire tunnel?

She squinted into the darkness and realized what that squealing, cracking noise had been—an entire wall of rock had fallen in, effectively blocking their exit. Abi didn't know of another way out except the entrance Grace was standing in front of.

Abi also knew Grace was ready to die before she let them pass.

She drew a long deep, calming breath, trying to formulate a plan without taking her eyes off Grace. Abi knew Grace hadn't killed her because she would be negotiating power if her plan upstairs didn't work and Asher survived, and for her part Abi wasn't going to kill Grace because she didn't know what that detonator in her hand was capable of. They were at a standoff.

She looked past Emilia and Alistair. She didn't see a way out, but she did see something she'd missed before: Alistair kept tilting his head to the side. At first she'd just thought he was uncomfortable, or it was a sign of nerves, but now that she looked more closely she realized it was more of a gesture. And if anyone knew these tunnels well, it would be him.

Abi followed his direction and her heart leapt in her chest when she saw a thin chasm in the tunnel wall. Abi had no idea where it would lead, but that chasm was an ember of hope.

Okay, so how were they going to disarm Grace?

Abi's eyes met Alistair's and he looked up.

Her eyes flickered to the ceiling, following Alistair's gaze, before immediately returning to Grace. She'd seen a water pipe, but didn't know what he was thinking to do with it. Shoot it? It might create some hysteria, perhaps enough to distract Grace and get the detonator from her hand . . .

Abi was thinking through all the possibilities and outcomes of attempting as much when she suddenly realized that wasn't what Alistair had been motioning to.

Her jaw set. She would only need a few seconds, but she also knew if this plan failed, Grace would almost certainly blow up the palace.

Abi prayed she wasn't making a mistake, but they didn't have a lot of options right now.

She brought her left hand to her cheek, resting her index finger on it. She hoped she looked thoughtful, or anxious—either would work—but regardless, Abi needed to give Alistair some warning because he would need to move fast.

She tapped her cheek once, then paused.

She tapped her cheek twice, then paused.

Then Abi whipped her pistol forward and shot the glass panel above Grace's head.

She fired five bullets in, not sure how strong the glass was, but within seconds it shattered, raining over Grace just as Alistair grabbed his mother, diving out of the way while Abi shot the guards beside them.

Abi turned back to Grace, gun raised, breathing heavily—only to see that she was retreating to where she had entered the tunnel. Abi knew she could either follow her, or they could escape before they were trapped. She decided on the latter—Thomas Security could deal with Grace when they had a spare moment. Right now, she needed to get everyone out before the tunnels collapsed in on them.

"Go!" Abi screamed, pointing toward the chasm.

They darted toward the area she had pointed to, Emilia and Alistair getting there first.

"Go! Go!" Abi urged them through as she sprinted toward them. More gunfire sounded from the end of the tunnel. Abi pushed her legs harder as her lungs burned for air. She squeezed in after Rachel and ignored the immediate pinch in her chest.

Breathe, Abi.

Her body scraped against the rock walls and if the wall had been a mirror, her breath would've fogged it she was so close.

She felt a prickle in her throat and it grew with every step.

"Keep moving forward!" Rachel said, and Abi wondered if that was directed at her.

Abi's shirt snagged and she tripped on her own feet, brushing her cheek against the rock. She wheezed in a breath and tried to put her hand on her chest, but the gap was too small. Panic rose in her chest and she knew she was on the verge of a panic attack.

You're fine. Breathe. You're fine. Breathe.

She repeated the mantras in her head with every step forward. She tilted her head back, but that was a mistake. Her chin scraped against the wall and her chest flared with panic.

She pushed it back down, refusing to succumb.

In what felt like ten hours but was likely only a minute or two, the chasm began to open up and Abi's lungs with it.

She burst through the opening, gasping for air as she leaned forward, resting her hands on her knees to catch her breath—but Rachel grabbed hold of her hand and pulled her forward. "We have to keep moving," she said with urgency.

Abi agreed mentally, but physically her lungs were still fighting to breathe.

Her legs were slow and moved like they didn't belong to her. She drew in deep breaths, trying to calm her racing pulse. When Abi saw the stairs ahead, she almost buckled.

Emilia was first up, her footsteps light and easy. Alistair was right behind her.

Rachel grabbed Abi around the waist and took most of her weight as they ran up the stairs.

Emilia had the door open when they arrived and Abi squinted as she stepped into the bright, white light.

"Where are we?" she asked, looking around, dazed and confused.

"Servants' quarters," Emilia said as she ran forward, leading the way.

But they were less than a few steps in when the familiar sound of gunfire echoed through the hallway and the walls around them started chipping.

"Left!" Emilia commanded and Abi skidded around the corner, her legs coming back to life.

They surged forward and Abi's heart was in her throat. As they came barreling around a corner, they saw a group of men at the end of the hallway.

"Next door!" Abi yelled and they rushed toward it. They ran inside and Abi locked the door.

"Window! Go!" Abi commanded as she attempted to drag the mahogany desk toward the door. Her lungs burned, but she refused to give up.

Alistair was beside her, hauling the table toward the door while Emilia unlocked the window.

They ran to the window and Abi kicked the screen out. She jumped through, checked the courtyard was secure, and then helped Emilia, Rachel, and Alistair through.

"There's a panic room. This way!" Alistair said, pointing at the door across the paved courtyard. The courtyard didn't look familiar to Abi; she wouldn't have been able to place herself on a map of the palace. But Alistair and Emilia could.

They sprinted forward as the pavers chipped beside them.

Abi stumbled, looking over her shoulder as she ran, and saw two men on the rooftop.

"Zigzag!" Abi shouted, but her order came too late. She screamed as fire spread over her arm, but somehow her feet managed to keep moving.

Emilia reached the window first and slammed her elbow into the glass.

She's really getting the hang of this, Abi thought. The thought left her mind as quickly as it came when Emilia's blood-curdling scream stopped her in her tracks.

"Going somewhere?" a man said as he stood on the other side of the window, inside the building. When Abi met his eyes, he smiled.

"Hello again," he said, his smile widening into an expression that would haunt her forever.

ABI

*A*bi heard the sound of guns cocking behind her and saw that two men had a pistol at Rachel's head. Emilia stood in front of them, her hands raised in surrender.

Abi's eyes darted between them all, frantic.

She stared at the ground, noticing the cracks in the pavement. She needed something to focus on—anything—to calm her mind.

Think, Abi. Think.

She was not giving up without a fight, but she didn't have only herself to think about.

"Let them go. Use me for leverage," Abi said and the man gave a smile that sent a shiver down Abi's spine.

"No one is going anywhere. Especially not him," he said, looking to Alistair.

"You won't succeed," Abi said through gritted teeth.

"There are armies on every border now. Your king made the mistake of thinking he was powerful. He tried to ruin Adani, and now he'll have to make a choice. If he chooses you and his family, the armies will cross the border and slaughter every Santinian in their path. If he chooses Santina, you all die." His lips curled up. "Your king will fall, because he cannot win—no matter what choice he makes from here on, he loses."

He raised his weapon and pointed it at Abi's forehead.

Abi held his gaze, refusing to back down, and desperately wished she had an earpiece. Where was Asher? What was happening?

She was still trying to formulate a plan when blood sprayed from the man's forehead and he dropped to the floor. Abi dropped to the ground, sheltering her head with her hands as a war erupted in the courtyard. She didn't know whether to run or to lie flat on the ground. But when she saw Jesse walking toward them with a thick layer of blood down one side of his face and six men behind him, Abi made her choice.

She jumped to her feet, pulled her weapon, and fired at the men on the rooftop.

"Inside!" Jesse screamed over the gunfire. Emilia, Alistair, and Rachel scrambled toward the door Jesse had just come from.

But they only made it a few steps.

Gunshots fired from the rooftops and Abi's heart pounded against her chest as she stayed where she was, firing at anything moving on the rooftop. When she saw them run inside, she could breathe again.

Jesse reached into his back pocket, pulled something out, and hurled into the sky.

"Down!" he said, knocking her to the ground as an explosion thundered through the courtyard. Jesse pulled her up and they scrambled back, taking shelter in the loggia.

"Where is everyone?" Abi screamed over the high-pitched whine in her ears. "Where are all the teams?"

"The palace is under siege," Jesse yelled back. "Everyone is cornered and being held!"

"And Asher?" Abi asked quickly as the ringing started to slowly fade from her ears.

"With James!" Jesse said. "Now, I need you to focus. Put this in," he ordered, handing her an earpiece.

Abi grabbed it gratefully, pushing it into her ear.

"*Good work, Abi,*" came Samuel's voice over the noise. "*I'm going to direct you now.*"

"Okay," Abi said shakily, then looked to Jesse. "What are you going to do?"

"Kill those bastards on the roof," he said grimly. "I'll see you at the meeting point Samuel creates." There was a promise in his eyes, but Abi couldn't begin to fathom the number of circumstances outside of his control right now.

"*On my command, run to the second window on your right. Three, two, one. Go!*" Samuel said as another explosion crackled through the air.

Abi's heart leapt into her throat as she sprinted for the window. Her legs felt light, fueled by adrenaline. She stole one quick look over her shoulder and saw the palace rooftop on fire.

She tried to open the window but it was locked. Slamming the butt of the pistol into the glass, she climbed through, hissing as her leg caught on the shards left behind.

After getting through, she briefly looked over the room—a sitting room of some kind, but she'd never been in this room before—and sprinted for the hallway, breathing hard. She scoped the hallway and decided it was clear, or clear enough.

"*Left!*" Samuel said.

She obeyed, sprinting as fast as her legs would carry her.

"*Take the next right, and then to the end of the hallway, straight down to the end. It's clear, but you need to move fast,*" Samuel said with urgency.

Abi pushed her legs faster and her lungs burned. Gunfire echoed so heavily it sounded like a thunderstorm, and it was coming from inside, of that she was sure.

"*Keep going, faster!*" Samuel said but Abi didn't think she could run any faster. She'd always been good at sports but admittedly she hadn't spent much time in a gym recently.

"*Go! Go! Go!*" Samuel said and as Abi skidded around the corner she saw why. There were two men behind her.

"*Next door on the left!*" Samuel said.

Abi almost tripped over her feet as she skidded on the polished concrete floor of the hallway. Samuel hadn't given her much notice.

She entered the room, an office, and looked around desperately.

"Right, into the living room and up the stairs. Go!"

Abi ran and took the steps two at a time, finding herself on a spiral staircase that never seemed to end.

"You're on level three," Samuel said as if he could read her mind.

Abi hadn't realized the palace even had three levels. Was she in the tower?

"Climb out the window."

Abi's heart skipped a beat, but it wasn't at Samuel's instructions. She heard footsteps on the stairs below her. She pressed on, unlocking the window and opening the window doors. She climbed through, swaying when she realized how high up she was.

"Run along the ledge, carefully. It's wide enough—and this is the only way out," Samuel told her, and it sounded like an apology.

Abi exhaled a shaky breath but when she saw a figure dart past the window, she knew she didn't have time to be nervous. She pressed her back flat against the wall, her fingertips gripping the thin moldings on the wall. She shuffled over but the ground beneath her swayed. She stopped, catching a breath that seemed to always escape her.

"Move," she whispered to herself as fear rose up in her throat—fear of falling, fear of dying, fear of never seeing Asher again.

"Keep going, just a few more—"

"Samuel?" Abi said, tapping the earpiece furiously. "Samuel?"

But the earpiece had gone quiet.

* * *

ASHER'S HEART drummed in his chest.

"James, four men at the end of the hallway. You need to retreat!" Samuel said through his earpiece.

James's head snapped in the opposite direction, but Asher couldn't see what he was looking at from his position inside. James pulled a mirror from his back pocket, using it to look around the doorframe.

Asher guessed they had a few seconds at most.

"Is the parallel hallway clear?" James asked quickly.

"Yes, from what I can see. Abi's on the rooftop. She'll be right above you," Samuel said, speaking so quickly Asher struggled to understand him.

"Stay in communication with Abi. Alert me if we're running into trouble. I'm taking Asher into the parallel hallway," James said.

James looked over his shoulder again and turned to face Asher. "We need to move. I need to get you into the other hallway, but we're going to have to run across the courtyard to get there," he said, gesturing to the window. "When I say go, sprint! Don't look around and don't stop if you hear gunfire. Run, and stay close to me!"

Asher nodded.

"Let's go!" James said as he closed the door, bolted it, and ran to the window, sliding it up, cutting out the screen.

He turned to Asher with focused eyes. "Ready?"

Asher swallowed the lump in his throat. "Ready."

"Go!" James said as he put one hand on the frame and jumped through the window. Asher mirrored him, eyed the door across the hallway and sprinted. Time seemed to slow down and his labored breath echoed like he was in a tunnel.

Asher almost stumbled as gunfire chipped the concrete path they were running on through the courtyard garden, but James turned and fired, not slowing down for a second.

Asher focused on the door, pushing his legs harder. He needed to get to Abi.

James raised his weapon again, this time firing at the window. It shattered and James made it to the window first, pulling his sleeve over his fist and opening a hole big enough for them to climb through.

"Put your foot on the ledge and climb in!"

Asher followed the instruction and jumped into the room. James followed him and sprinted to the doorway, checking that the hallway was clear.

"Let's go," James said. "We're going left, right to the end of the hallway, and then up the stairs."

Asher nodded as he ran forward.

"Go!" James said and they sprinted into the hallway.

The windows shattered as they ran, one by one, only a second behind Asher and James.

The glass seemed to be shattering before they passed it now and the end of the hallway didn't look to be getting any closer.

"Keep going!" James screamed, firing as he ran.

"Go, go, go!" James said as they reached the stairs, climbing them two at a time. Asher fought to breathe, to keep his mind calm, but it was getting harder with every step.

They sprinted through the hallway and into the formal dining hall.

They were almost at the tower when James skidded to a halt—and Asher's breath caught in his throat as six men with guns emerged from the kitchen.

ABI

"Keep moving. Come on, Abi," Samuel said. "*Grab the bars of the balcony and pull one knee up, and then the other and stand. You can do this.*"

She grabbed onto the black iron bars of the balcony and grunted as she pulled herself up. She managed to lift one knee, but she wasn't high enough, and she dropped down, panting.

"*Again, come on!*" Samuel said.

Abi took a deep breath and jumped up, hauling herself up, one knee on the ledge and then another. She stood, not daring to look down.

"*Shuffle toward the rooftop,*" Samuel said. Abi shuffled across, breathing hard, fighting the panic constricting her throat. She made it around to the edge without falling and climbed onto the adjoining rooftop.

The last time she'd been running on rooftops it had been dark, and she'd only been one or two stories high. But now she was three or four—she couldn't even remember—and she could see the ground below. She felt unbalanced and shaky on her feet.

"*Run!*" Samuel shouted and Abi surged forward with no idea of where she was going. She heard glass shattering below her but didn't stop to look.

She ran as fast as she could, careful not to slip or lose her balance on the roof tiles. She risked another look down, but the ground seemed to blur below her. She kept her attention up, focused on where to place her feet.

"*Stop! Go back!*" Samuel yelled, and Abi's head snapped up to see two men climbing up onto the rooftop.

She spun around, running the way she'd come but she'd only taken a few steps before she saw a man climb up to the rooftop, blocking her path. He held an automatic weapon in his hand.

"Stop!" the man commanded and Abi came to a halt. She looked between the men, frantically searching for a way out but she was trapped.

The man closest to her took a step forward, and then another.

Abi choked on her breath. Unless she slid down the side of the building, they would capture her. And she was almost certain she wouldn't make it to the edge before they shot at her.

"Samuel . . ." Abi said warily, unsure exactly what Samuel could do to help her right now.

"*Don't move. Stall them,*" he said, his words laced with determination.

She looked over the edge of the building. It was a long drop to the ground, but it might be her only option.

"Drop your weapon," the man commanded.

Abi raised her hands in surrender as she took a look over her shoulder at the man behind her. He was moving fast. She only had a few seconds to make a decision.

She looked down again, hoping she'd be able to use the moldings on the wall to lower down, but she wasn't hopeful.

Bending her knees, she pretended to surrender. Her weapon was on the ground and the man was closing fast when she heard the echo of gunfire.

The man in front of her fell, and then a second shot fired and Abi looked over her shoulder at the other man—also down.

She grabbed her weapon and jumped to her feet as she looked over the rooftop and saw someone running toward her. He was impossibly light on his feet, and she knew who it was: Reed.

Abi sprinted in his direction, never so happy to see him.

"Tower!" Reed shouted and pointing as he surged forward.

Abi turned and ran parallel with Reed, heading for the tower in front of them. She hurdled over the fallen man, but her foot caught on a broken tile. She fell, reaching out her hands. Pain shot through her palms as she landed and it took her a moment to clear her head and jump up again. She ran forward, but everything ached. Her body was tired and sore and she was sick of running, but right now she didn't have a choice. She set her eyes on the tower, refusing to focus on anything else. She blocked the pain, the fatigue, and the fear from her mind.

Reed reached the tower before her, but she was only a few seconds behind. He fired at the lock on the door and then yanked it open. The lights activated as they stepped inside and ran down the stairs. Reed checked the hallway, and then motioned her forward. "Slowly," he said with a hushed voice.

Abi took a calming breath but her eyes darted to the ticking wall clock that sounded impossibly loud and had to be all in her mind. She shook her head, the irony not lost on her.

Focus, Abi.

Reed peered around the corner and then righted, like he'd seen someone, and Abi held her breath, not daring to make a sound.

She stayed still, not moving an inch, but her heart slammed against her ribs as if it were trying to escape without her.

Suddenly, Reed stepped around the corner, raised his weapon and fired before screaming, "Go!"

ASHER

Panic flowed through his body like a poison.

James skidded to a halt but he didn't lower his weapon.

Asher looked around, frantic. There were men behind them and in front of them. Every hallway they turned down, they were met with more men. Asher didn't know how many bullets James had left, but it couldn't be many.

"When I yell 'down,' look at your feet and close your eyes," James said under his breath.

"Okay," Asher said as James threw a black ball into the air.

"Down," James said and Asher squeezed his eyes shut. He heard a loud bang and then James was pulling on his arm, tugging him through the closest door.

They ran at full speed through the library. James stopped at a bookcase and leaned in, grunting as he pushed it.

Asher's eyebrows lifted as the bookcase turned, revealing a secret door. "I had no idea this was here," he said, confused.

"It wasn't until we arrived," James said with a tight grin. "Go!"

Asher darted inside to see a wooden staircase that had been built into it, leading down to the floor below. "You've been busy," he said as he ran down the stairs.

"Just taking precautions," James replied. "Follow me," he said as they stepped off the last step. He turned to the door and slowly turned the knob, paused again to listen, then peered around the corner.

"Clear," he said quietly—perhaps for his team's benefit.

He held up two fingers, curling them toward the door, motioning them forward.

James led the way with Asher right behind him. Asher found himself in the storeroom for the maintenance staff. James grabbed a bottle off the shelf and poured it behind them, creating a trail, then grabbed a small pair of shears.

Asher had no idea what was going on.

They crept forward, barely making a sound. It had been a long time since Asher had been down there so he'd lost his sense of direction. He had no idea which way they were headed.

"We're near the panic room," James said as if he could read Asher's mind. "Abi is there with your mother and Alistair. My teams have taken control of the east and north wings. I'll come back for you when the palace has been cleared—" James's head snapped to the left and he ran to a desk against the wall. "Samuel, a command center was set up in the maintenance store room. Review all related footage."

"*Copy*," Samuel said as a figure emerged from behind a storage rack beside James.

Before Asher could yell out to him, James spun around, pushing the shears into the man's stomach. The man grunted, falling to his knees before falling forward. Asher grimaced at the sickening sound he made as his body hunched over, propped up only by the shears.

James returned his attention to the desk, searching it quickly. He looked to the shelf, tucked something into his pocket, and then ran back to Asher.

"We need to move," he said. "That guy was running some sort of command center. When he stops communicating, they're going to realize he's down and someone—or a team—will come to replace him."

James, not waiting for Asher, darted his eyes from side to side, searching for something. He pressed up suddenly, grabbing a small bottle from the shelf before filling it with the chemical he had picked up earlier.

"This way," he said, setting the larger container to the side while he screwed on the lid of the smaller bottle.

Asher nodded and James went ahead, scoping between the storage units then motioning Asher forward. They moved as fast as they could, but James seemed even more alert than usual.

They ran into the service elevator and Asher got his bearings. James pressed level one. When they emerged from the elevator, they had to make it down two hallways to reach the panic room.

The doors opened and James held up his hand, signaling to wait. He crept forward, pressing the button to keep the doors open.

James held a finger to his lips and then pointed to Asher's right.

Asher's pulse continued to race, but the longer they were running, the less frantic it was. He didn't know if the adrenaline was wearing off or if it was fatigue settling in.

They moved quickly—not quite running, but not walking either—and they were almost at the end of the hallway when Asher heard footsteps behind them.

James spun around, pulled a box of matches from his pocket, lit one and threw it on the ground. Only when a line of flames flickered before them did Asher realize what that bottle James was carrying had in it, and why he'd been trailing it behind them.

Asher couldn't see what was happening, but he heard their chaotic cries.

"Retreat!" a voice called out, but judging by the sound of the agonized screams that followed, Asher assumed some of them didn't move fast enough.

Their victory was short lived as another group of men barreled around the corner, backing them against the flames.

James fired through the flames, making sure no one retreated.

"King Asher," one man said with a smug grin.

Asher met his gaze, refusing to back down. "How will your family feel when they learn you attempted to assassinate the king? They will be rejected from their communities. You have brought shame to Santina, and Santina will not forgive you."

James spun around, keeping his weapon raised. But they were outnumbered.

"Not all of Santina stands behind you, Your Majesty," he said with a hint of self-righteousness.

"I do," came a familiar voice as Asher saw Alistair emerge from the intersecting hallway.

Alistair fired shots into the men as he strode forward.

Asher screamed as he saw the men turn, raising their weapons at his brother.

He could see what was happening, but he was powerless to stop it.

Gunfire erupted and Asher's world stopped as Alistair's body jerked before he fell.

The men in front of Asher fell as James fired and Asher lunged for his brother.

"Alistair!" he said, grabbing his brother's hand and lifting his head. His gaze dropped to the blood-soaked T-shirt covering his abdomen. "Hang on! Don't you dare give up on me!"

Alistair managed a weak smile. "Maybe Santina will be proud of me now," he said, his breathing shallow.

Asher's eyes pricked hot tears. "Santina is proud of you. *I* am proud of you!" he told his brother quickly.

Alistair's eyes lit up before they rolled back in his head.

"Alistair!" Asher screamed as a team of men swarmed around them.

James kneeled on the ground beside Alistair. "Sit back, I need room," he said quickly as he lifted Alistair's T-shirt, pressing his hand on the wound. "Pass me a kit!" he commanded and one of his men dropped to the ground beside him, opening a black bag.

"Clotting patch," James commanded, holding out his hand. A white fabric strip was passed to him and as he lifted his hand to apply it, blood bubbled out, pooling on the floor. James ripped the backing off the patch and stuck it onto Alistair's skin, holding his hand over it.

"Samuel, I need to get him to a hospital," James said quickly, his eyes never leaving Alistair's wound.

"Paramedics are moving in now. Backup teams are scoping the palace. So far it's clean."

Alistair mumbled something and Asher leaned in.

"What did you say?" Asher asked. "What did you say?" he repeated, his words desperate, but Alistair only gave him a wide smile as his body began to shake.

"Alistair! Stay with me!" Asher screamed.

ASHER

*A*sher watched helplessly as a team of men lifted Alistair and carried him away. He'd been told they would meet the paramedics and rush him to the hospital.

"We need to keep moving," James told him.

Asher's eyes dropped to the pool of blood on the floor. "How did he know we were trapped?"

James shook his head. "He didn't. He left the panic room a few minutes ago saying he wasn't going to sit and do nothing, and for once, Alistair was in the right place at the right time."

"Let's go," James said, stepping over the pool of blood.

They ran down the hallway, flanked by a team of men. James entered a code on the door and guided Asher inside the moment it opened.

His eyes landed on Abi and his composure cracked. Her cheek was grazed, there was blood in her hair, and by the way she was holding her arm, he knew she'd been injured. But she stood and rushed toward him.

He held out his arms, wrapping her up, holding her close.

"Are you okay?" he asked.

"Yes," she said, her words muffled against his chest.

Asher kissed the crown of her head and drew a long deep breath for the first time since the masked man had stormed his office.

He opened his eyes and his gaze settled on his mother, who was watching them with a smile. Asher's heart broke, realizing he knew he would have to tell her about Alistair.

"Give me a second," he said under his breath as Abi pulled back.

She dropped her arms and he brushed a thumb over her cheek before he strode toward his mother. "Are you hurt?" he asked, kneeling in front of her.

"No," she said, shaking her head. "Are you?"

"No," Asher said. "Alistair saved my life today, and he was shot. They've rushed him to the hospital, but he's going to be fine."

His mother's face turned white and the sparkle in her eyes faded.

"He's going to be fine," Asher repeated, as much to convince his mother as himself.

"He's in the ambulance now," Reed broke in. "He's stable."

Asher nodded gratefully, letting out a breath he didn't know he'd been holding in. "Thank you."

"We're doing a final sweep of the palace and then we're going to move you all out. We've spoken to the Bennetts and we're going to use their home as a base until we can secure another. It has a great surveillance and security system," Reed added.

"Okay," Asher said blankly as James Thomas walked in. Asher noted his bloodstained hands, and his mind returned to his brother.

Keep fighting, Alistair.

"You have a problem," James said.

Asher's eyebrows lifted. "What now?"

"I have confirmation that Adani soldiers are on every border surrounding Santina," he said.

Asher leaned forward like James had kicked him in the stomach.

"How many soldiers?" he asked with a strained voice.

"Samuel estimates about two hundred thousand men," James replied.

Asher fought to breathe. "I need a secure phone line."

"Talk to me, Asher," James said calmly. "Tell me what's going through your head."

"Santina doesn't have a big enough army. I can't fight Adani, not on my own. So I'm going to request . . . no, beg," Asher clarified. He was not above begging at this point. He began to pace. "Beg the others to fight with us, with Santina. I'll show the neighboring kingdoms the poisoning evidence and what Adani is capable of, including the development of biological warfare weapons. If they want to protect their kingdoms, I'm their best shot."

Asher looked at James, his eyes going hard. "I didn't want to go to war, not like this, but I won't back down if my hand is forced."

* * *

JAMES SPENT the next thirty minutes coordinating with William's private security team and William authorized Samuel to take full control of the security system. When he'd given permission for Samuel to run checks on all his staff, Samuel had faltered. It turned out Thomas Security had taken that liberty upon themselves after Abi's kidnapping and all of William's staff passed their assessment.

As they drove through the main gates, Asher realized he'd never even seen a photograph of the Bennett family home. It wasn't a royal palace, but it came in a close second. It must've been the largest residential home in Santina, which wasn't surprising given the family's wealth, but the fact that they'd managed to keep photographs of it off the internet was impressive.

"Did you grow up in this house?" he asked, turning to Abi.

"I did," she said casually.

The car came to a stop and they were ushered inside. William stood, ready to greet them. He extended his hand to Asher. "You've had a rough day."

"It's not over yet," Asher said grimly.

William turned his attention to his daughter and his face fell. "I'm starting to think you're a cat with nine lives."

Abi gave a small smile. "I'm fine, I promise."

"Thank you for having us—all of us," Asher clarified, aware that there were at least thirty people standing behind him.

Asher's eyes swept over the home as they walked through the hallways, but he didn't really see it. His mind was lost in the details of what had to happen next.

William led them to his personal office. "I'll leave you to it."

"Thank you," Asher said, staring at the desk that reminded him of his own. He wondered what the palace's damage bill would be, and then decided he didn't want to know. He had enough to focus on right now.

James passed him his cell phone, which had been swept and tested again to make sure it hadn't been tapped. "Make the call," he said with a nod.

Asher scrolled through the contacts until he found the one he was looking for.

His pulse was strong and steady as he waited for the call to be answered.

"King Asher. This is a surprise," King Khalil said cautiously.

"Because you thought I'd be dead by now?" Asher asked flatly. "You know why I'm calling, and I'm giving you one chance to stand down your soldiers. If they cross into Santina, there will be a war—and I will destroy you," he said, his voice a growl.

"You are full of threats, King Asher," King Khalil hissed. "But you forget one thing: you have a small army. We are Adani!"

"And Adani just attempted regicide," Asher said firmly. "Make no mistake, my threats are not empty. If one Adani soldier steps over into Santina, we will fight back. You think Santina is weak, you think I am weak, but let me tell you this: you will be like a deer caught in headlights if you make the mistake of stepping foot in my kingdom. Your fear will asphyxiate you, and I will not give you mercy."

"If you fight me, I will slaughter every innocent Santinian in my path, the entire way to your palace. Good luck, King Asher," he said smugly before ending the call.

Asher looked at the phone, grinding his teeth. "Get the helicopter ready."

James nodded and drew his phone, stepping outside to make the calls.

Asher looked to Abi. He needed to hear what had happened in the tunnels, but he didn't have time right now and he felt guilty about that.

He sighed as he sat beside her on the couch. "Abi, I need to leave and sort this out. We're going to war."

She bit her lip, nodding hesitantly. He understood. She was a humanitarian, she saved lives, and now he was going to start a war where many innocent lives would be lost.

"Asher, the helicopter is ready," James's voice broke in.

"Give me a minute," he said, not taking his eyes off Abi.

"Sure," James said, and Asher heard the door close.

Abi looked back to him. "I know this isn't what you wanted, Asher. But I know this is what you have to do. If Adani storms Santina, it will fall. We have to fight back," she said, shaking her head as her mind and heart clearly fought against each other.

Asher nodded, returning his attention to Abi. "I need to go and meet with our allies. It's time to end Adani."

"Go," Abi said without hesitation. "Go and teach them Santina is stronger than they'll ever be."

He kissed her forehead, letting his lips linger for a second, and then stepped back.

James was waiting outside for him. "Alistair is in emergency surgery. He's stable and they think he'll make a full recovery."

Asher drew a calming breath, trying to clear his mind. He was worried about Alistair, and he was worried about leaving Abi and his mother—if the palace could be attacked, the Bennetts' house could be too.

Asher knew that if that happened, and he was at the house, there would be little he could do to protect her. But he'd still want to be there. As tragic as his father's death had been, there was one factor Asher had found comforting—he'd died next to his wife. He hadn't died alone.

He shook his head, needing to get a grip on his mind. Abi was with her family and there was no way William Bennett would go down without a fight. Not to mention, James was extremely impressed with the security system for their house.

He followed James into the elevator and pushed down his anxiety that was rising faster than the elevator. When they stepped out onto the rooftop, William's private helicopter was waiting for them with its propellers slicing through the air.

They ran toward it and climbed inside. Asher was barely buckled in when the helicopter tilted as it began to hover.

Asher gripped the arm rests—he hated helicopters, he always had, but they provided an efficient means of transport and they could land where he needed them to.

"Flight time, approximately one hour," the pilot said.

Asher pulled out his phone, needing a distraction from the slight turbulence as the helicopter reached full height. He stole one quick look out the window at his kingdom below.

The sun was climbing in the sky but Santina was just waking up. Some homes had lights on, visible through the hazy dawn light. But others were still asleep. Asher wondered if they were sleeping soundly —and wondered when he'd sleep like that again.

He returned his attention to his phone and the emails that were flooding his inbox. He'd spoken individually to every ruler of Santina's allying kingdoms. He'd advised them Adani had attempted regicide, had infiltrated their kingdoms, and had men stationed on the border they shared with Santina. That had been enough to agree to an emergency confidential meeting, an assembly of kingdoms— excluding Adani.

Asher typed furiously, needing every minute to prepare for this meeting. Realistically, he needed a week. But he was only going to get . . . fifty-eight minutes he realized, looking at the time on his phone.

Asher knew he wouldn't stick to a prepared speech—he never had —but he needed a list of everything he wanted to discuss, because he couldn't leave anything out. This kind of meeting had never occurred before, and Asher had to make sure he utilized every opportunity that would come from it, because what he would ask them to do at the conclusion of the meeting was unprecedented.

Asher was still typing on his phone when the helicopter landed on the pad at Umaid Palace, owned by King Luang—the King of Valencia.

Asher looked out to see Luang waiting for them, accompanied by three rows of security.

Asher might've been intimidated by the amount of security except for one fact: King Martin and King Luang had always had a good relationship, and that relationship was the primary reason Asher had asked King Luang to host this emergency assembly.

With James Thomas beside him, Asher walked toward the king and extended his hand.

The king's handshake was firm and his smile warm. His dark brown eyes were welcoming—as if greeting an old friend. Asher might've been intimidated by his security, but Luang himself was a different story. He reminded Asher of his own grandfather—he even had a similar, stocky build—but Asher wasn't fooled by his appearance. King Luang was well respected for both his intelligence and his strategic moves. His kingdom had flourished under his rule, and they had gone from impoverished to wealthy in a matter of decades.

"Everyone is assembled in the cabinet room," King Luang said. "They are anxiously awaiting your arrival, Your Majesty."

"Best not keep them waiting, then," Asher said, noting the glimmer in King Luang's eyes.

"I wish your father could see you right now," he said with a sad smile.

"I hope he can," Asher said.

They turned and walked toward the door leading into the palace.

"Asher, I'm hesitant to give you advice on this without knowing the full extent of why you've requested this meeting. But you have to know there are some kingdoms that will not go against Adani. They rely on Adani, much like Santina once did," King Luang said quietly.

"I know, and that's why I only invited our allies. If everyone here today agrees, we will defeat Adani," Asher said stridently.

King Luang's fluffy eyebrows lifted high on his forehead. He rubbed his palms together. "This I can't wait to see."

Asher's heart began to beat a little faster and his hands were sweaty. This would be the biggest negotiation of his life, and he had one chance to make it happen.

King Luang entered first and the group hushed, standing for his arrival.

But their eyes were on Asher.

ASHER

Asher looked over two the men and one woman assembled. The Adani ruler was noticeably absent.

Asher looked to King Luang, who motioned for them to sit before nodding to Asher.

His hand went to his tie, which felt like it was choking him, but he refrained from touching it, choosing to smooth out his jacket instead. He could not appear weak. Not now, not ever—not in front of these leaders.

Asher cleared his throat. "Thank you for making the effort to meet here today, especially given the late notice and lack of information provided to you."

Heads nodded and Asher continued.

"The Kingdom of Santina has been in an invisible war with Adani for the past few years, which came to light after the murder of my father. Adani is bold, and they fear nothing—including the law. They will destroy whomever they want, and they will take whatever they want, at any cost," Asher said gravely. "I'm here today because a few hours ago, Adani attacked my palace, shot my brother, attempted to kill me, my fiancée, and my mother, and has lined every border of Santina with Adani soldiers. Their plan to kill us failed, so now King

Khalil has given me a demand: back down to his army and let them take Santina, or they will slaughter every innocent Santinian in their path. That was his biggest mistake."

All eyes were on Asher.

"I know this is hard to believe, so I am going to play you a recording of the phone conversation," Asher said. He looked at James and nodded.

The recording began to play and Asher took a deep breath. He could hear the anger in his own voice.

When it finished, he said, "I will give you a copy if you'd like, so you can see the recording has not been edited."

He looked over the gathering, a small but powerful group. "Adani has secrets buried so deep they are sleeping on top of them," Asher continued. "They shouldn't be able to close their eyes at night, but they can—and they do—because they fear no one. They have become too powerful," he said, and then took a calming breath. "I know that many of you in this room rely on Adani for aid. I understand that, as Santina was in that same position not too long ago. But I ask you to watch this video with an open mind, because this doesn't just affect Adani—it affects all of our kingdoms and the entire world."

Asher nodded again, indicating for the video to be played.

This time King Khalil's face flashed up on the wall.

"What do you mean our system was hacked?" the king asked.

"We detected a breach on the system and we followed it—they were looking at our financial records."

The king paused, rubbing the back of his neck.

"Can we trace the location of the hacker?"

"We're working on it."

The Adani king looked to the man he was speaking with. *"I'll bet it was Asher's new security team . . . I will teach them a lesson. Are we ready to contaminate Santina's water supply?"*

"We're ready. We have created a bacteria that is twice as potent as the one used on our system previously."

"And you are one hundred percent sure the weaknesses of your previous

specimen have been corrected, right?" the king asked. "Make sure they can't treat this with an antibiotic."

"This will be fatal and limited to Santina. There will be no stopping it."

"When will it be ready?"

"Two months."

The king nodded. "Begin. Asher managed to foil our other plans, but he won't be able to stop this. And find out where that hacker is. I want to send him a gift," he said with a haunting grin.

The video recording paused.

Asher looked over the wide eyes assembled before him.

"The Adani system was hacked at my command," Asher admitted, knowing he'd broken the law and could be punished for it. "But, I wasn't looking at their financial records. I was looking for information on another human rights case that my father had always thought Adani guilty of, but didn't have proof. I couldn't find proof of that, or anything in their system, either. But what I did instruct my hacker to do was feed their system back to ours. I didn't plant cameras in the king's office—they were already there. But I laid a trap for him . . . we intentionally left a trace in their system so they knew they had been hacked, and then we tapped his cameras."

Asher held the gazes of Santina's allies. "I know this was illegal, but my country is being attacked and my father has been murdered in an act of regicide. At the same time, I have been continuously threatened and blackmailed. I cannot stand by and let this happen, as I doubt anyone in this room could. None of this information has been released outside this room, and this is the reason I asked for this meeting—so that I could show it to you without risking the intelligence being intercepted by anyone.

"Now, there is one more video I'd like to show you," Asher said, and all eyes returned to the wall.

A video of the laboratory began playing. The audio wasn't great quality, but it was just good enough to overhear the sound bite.

"Santina is first, followed by Valencia. We'll further refine the bacteria after we see the live results."

At this, Asher met King Luang's blazing eyes.

"What do you propose we do, Asher?" King Luang asked.

This was the moment of truth. Would they side with him, or would they back Adani out of fear?

"These videos were recorded about a week ago, so we have a few weeks, maybe, to formulate a plan. My intention is to overthrow Adani," he said. Murmurs began to circulate, and he raised his hands placatingly. "But I need your help to do that. The king is right—Santina's army is not big enough to defeat Adani. Together, however, we have five hundred thousand soldiers and, with a good strategy, we can defeat them. But we must do this together."

Asher looked back to Luang. "When Adani falls, my suggestion, if King Luang agrees, is that King Luang and I will take joint sovereign control of the land, and every kingdom here today—all of you—will receive an equal share of the income that will continue to be generated from Adani's oil wells. You are reliant on Adani for financial aid, but that would no longer be true if you received a portion of their income each year.

"Sovereign control is complicated, and having too many parties involved will only make it more so," Asher continued. "Therefore, while it is my preference to work alongside King Luang should he agree, I am willing for this assembly to take a confidential vote. If you wish for someone else to lead Adani's people, I am willing to step aside."

Asher looked at each one in turn. "It is not my objective to take over Adani because of power or greed. I never wanted to be the King of Santina! But, I do want to make sure that Adani doesn't destroy my kingdom, or any of yours—and I will spend the rest of my life fighting to make sure that doesn't happen. I want my family to be safe and to live without fear of being attacked in my own home. I want my people to not only eat and survive, but to thrive, and it has become increasingly clear that I can't do that while Adani exists as it does today."

His gaze swept across the room. "Adani does not care about my people—the fact that they are willing to slaughter every innocent Santinian in their path proves that—but they do care about the oil underneath a holy site in my land . . . a site my father refused to test, because he would never have allowed the site to be ruined for financial gain."

The eyes of the other leaders stayed locked on Asher.

"So, you can stand beside me today and see your kingdom thrive under a new leadership of the lands of Adani . . . or you can continue to live as you are: praying like hell that Adani doesn't turn on you and you don't end up in my situation."

The room was silent—likely because they all knew, like Asher knew, that while it was a good plan, if they failed, Adani would destroy them all.

Finally, King Luang stood and broke the silence. "I am willing to stand beside you Asher, and I would be willing to lead Adani with you —however that looks. In the interest of this gathering, though I believe we should cast confidential votes. This way, everyone has their say; and, if any of you decide you don't want to take a stand against Adani, then you can refuse to vote. But," King Luang said, looking over the men he'd known for much longer than Asher had, "I can't speak for Asher, but I can personally promise you this: if you don't stand against Adani, don't expect me to save you when they turn on you. Remember that King Martin, and Santina, were once one of Adani's greatest allies—"

"What you have done is illegal," one of the rulers interrupted bluntly, looking directly at Asher. "How do we know that we can trust you?"

Asher nodded. "You don't," he admitted. "But I ask that if you trusted my father, you place that same trust in me. I have every intention of continuing his legacy."

No one answered, but he saw their eyes soften slightly.

Asher continued, "If I wanted to play this to my own advantage, I could've leaked this on the internet. I could've sent it to a media source, who would've printed it in newspapers all over the world. It would've made me look like a hero. Instead, I chose to come to you— to all that are directly involved in this—so that we could decide together the best steps to take to ensure our people are safe. If my hand is forced, I will respond by whatever means necessary, but I don't act for my own benefit. I act because I vowed to protect my people," Asher said.

No one said anything, and Asher didn't know whether to sit or stand or what to say from there.

"I am an old man," King Luang said with an apologetic grin, "so we'll do this the old way. Write the names of the person, or people, you would like to see lead Adani and then bring it to me. I'll shuffle the papers in front of you, so you can see no papers are tampered with. And then we'll reveal the names on the papers together. If you choose not to side with us, leave your piece of paper blank and hand it in. Each vote will be anonymous. Any concerns or questions?"

The assembly looked to one another, but no one voiced any questions.

"Okay," King Luang said looking to an assistant, who scurried off —assumingly to find some paper and pens. Asher sat at the table, feeling like a child voting for a school project. Though Asher didn't care for the method—he wanted what was fair and what would give everyone a say.

The assistant returned with paper and pens, and Asher wrote his own name and King Luang's before folding it and handing it to the assistant.

Then he waited. But his mind was calm, as was his heart, because he'd spoken the truth—he was not interested in Adani for the power it would bring him. If anyone else in the room was elected to run it, he would be satisfied with that—it would mean fewer headaches and more time he could spend focused on Santina.

Paper after paper, the votes came in until King Luang stood and shuffled them with an ease that indicated he'd enjoyed a game or two of cards over the course of his life.

He looked over the group, and then opened the first paper.
King Luang.
King Asher.

Asher felt eyes watching him but he didn't react, because he truly didn't care. Everyone in the room was capable of leading Adani. Asher had offered to step up and lead the country because he'd started this conflict, and he would take responsibility for it. But sitting back, doing none of the work involved in Adani and taking a cut of their income every month . . . well, that was an enticing option. But it was the easy option, and he knew his father would never sit back and not put his hand up.

Asher heard his name over and over again until King Luang paused. The last piece of paper was blank. Due to the king's shuffling skills, Asher had no idea who had submitted it—but someone had chosen Adani.

And that meant that as soon as they were released from this room, there would be a phone call made to the Adani king.

ASHER

Everyone looked to one another, no one quite sure what to do next—including Asher. Something like this had never been done before.

"I know you have important responsibilities at home, but I ask you to remain here for a little longer so that we can consult with you on the next steps," Asher said, watching each of them carefully.

Asher's head snapped to the doorway as James Thomas interrupted him. "I'm sorry, but may I please speak with you privately?" he whispered.

"What is it?" Asher asked.

James's eyes darted over the assembly. "Santina has been breached on the border it shares with Arinia."

Asher turned to the one woman in the room, the one who had most to lose from the fall of Adani and the one Asher suspected didn't write anything on the paper.

The Queen of Arinia looked to James, either having heard him or guessing what he'd said. "I sent my soldiers there," she said.

"My understanding is that they never made it to the border. They were attacked about ten minutes ago," James responded.

Asher could see the betrayal in her eyes. She'd thought she was safe, but Asher knew no one was safe from Adani.

"I need to make a call," she said as she lifted her phone from the table. "Yes . . . how many . . . Adani?" A long pause followed and she visibly swallowed. "Send in every soldier. Tell them to protect Santina until King Asher can rally more troops. Protect the Santina citizens and move them into Arinia if you need to. Keep me updated." She put the phone down.

She closed her eyes for the briefest of moments. "I provided the blank piece of paper," she admitted, looking at no one in particular. "You aren't the only one being threatened, Asher."

Asher couldn't hide his surprise, and he was disgusted at the nerve of Adani—they thought they were untouchable.

"I change my vote," she continued. "You and King Luang have my full support. I put an additional hundred thousand soldiers on standby before this meeting. They will move in and work with your army to keep Adani out."

"Thank you," Asher said, at a loss for more adequate words. "How did he threaten you?"

"Money," she said simply. "Ninety percent of our funding comes from Adani now."

Asher's jaw dropped open. "Why?"

She sighed. "Three years ago, our agriculture was hit with a plague and it was wiped out. I'm sure you heard about this, but I downplayed the full extent of it to avoid panic amongst my people. Adani stepped in to offer aid, and they have continued to increase it since. Now I feel like a fool, because I'm beginning to doubt that plague was born of natural origins," she said. Asher respected the courage it took to admit as much so bluntly, particularly amongst a room of powerful rulers.

"I feel like a fool too," Asher admitted. "Adani has been infiltrating Santina for three years at least, likely more. I didn't see it, or perhaps I didn't want to. But that changes today. Today we stand up against the evil they have become. Today we take a stand for our people. We can only do this together."

She nodded but Asher saw the steely determination in her eyes.

"But how do we proceed?" another asked.

"We formulate a plan to obliterate Adani at every border, at the same time," Asher said slowly. "We use everything we have: men on the ground, planes, and bombs. And while that's happening, we'll hit the royal compound in Adani. My security team has offered to infiltrate Adani and be on the ground so when this happens, we make sure the king doesn't escape."

"That is a very well thought-out plan," the same man said.

Asher didn't know if that was criticism or a compliment. "That's what happens when I'm blackmailed and the people I love are hurt and murdered. My father told me to make decisions I can sleep with at night . . . and ruining King Khalil before he destroys our region is a decision I can live with. I did not want a war, and I did not want innocent lives to be lost, but they have given me—us—no choice." Asher swallowed the lump in his throat. "The loss of innocents is happening right now as we speak, but I will do everything in my power to ensure the lives lost are as few as possible. Even Adani lives—Adani civilians should not pay the price of their ruler's greed."

King Luang nodded with appreciative eyes. "I support this plan in its entirety. If no one objects"—no one raised a hand in dissent, and Luang nodded—"then let us proceed. We need to move fast."

The Queen of Arinia looked at her phone, then back up. "My men are assembled, King Asher. They're crossing the border into Santina now."

ASHER

Asher's stomach churned violently as the drone surveillance footage projected onto the screen. King Luang stood beside him, and the Queen of Arinia on the other. Asher didn't know if any of them were breathing as the sight of tens of thousands of soldiers filled the screen. Arinia's soldiers were passing through Santina's border control a few hundred miles from Adani's soldiers, who were lining the border at the mountains.

Asher knew this wouldn't be a quick fight—it would go on for months, maybe years—and he would need to lead Santina through it. He would need to keep his people calm and their morale high. Asher prayed he could do that because right now, looking at the screens, he felt like he was suffocating. He wondered if his father would still be proud of him. He'd fought so hard to avoid a war, and now Asher was marching into one within a few months of his father's death.

Asher shook his head. So much had changed since his father's death—because of his father's death—and Adani wasn't prepared to stay in the shadows any longer. They wanted Santina, and Asher would die before he let that happen.

The tanks rolled over the border, the Arinian soldiers marching beside them.

The queen looked to Asher, and he hoped his face was a picture of calm—the very opposite of what he felt.

She returned her attention to the screen and Asher fought to exhale calmly.

The footage on the screen split into four screens, each one at a Santinian border. Asher tracked the Arinian soldiers with his gaze, following them into Santina where they split off, separating into two units. One unit tracked along the border, ready to fight the Adani soldiers, and the second unit headed for the city, dropping soldiers at every village on their path to protect Santina's citizens from counter-attacks. The plan was to hit Adani from inside Santina's border, forcing them back.

Four allies, four kingdoms of soldiers, and Santina's army was everything he had, and Asher prayed it was enough.

King Luang's Commander-in-Chief was coordinating their strategy, and when every soldier was in position, he commanded them to attack.

The tanks fired at the borders, lighting up the ink-blue sky.

Asher crossed his arm over his chest as that strange feeling of not knowing who he was anymore settled in.

He'd just started a war.

He'd known what he was doing, of course, but the reality had just hit him and the weight of that decision—one that he could never go back from—was strangling. He'd told the Adani king—King Khalil—he was going to asphyxiate him with fear, but Asher wondered if he'd just asphyxiated himself.

Over and over again, the tanks fired and Adani retaliated. The commander was receiving communication from each unit on the ground and had full decision-making power to make the calls. Asher wasn't going to pretend to be a war strategist, but he trusted King Luang, and King Luang's commander had been to war before—and won.

"It's unsettling, isn't it?" King Luang asked, eyeing him carefully. "I remember being in your position, the first time I led my kingdom to war. I was older than you, but I'm not sure that makes the decision any easier. War is war, and there's nothing nice about it."

"No, there's not," Asher agreed as the commander issued a string of orders to various teams.

The sun rose on the horizon, bringing light to the decisions they'd made last night. With each minute the sun rose higher, the immediate toll the war was taking became evident. Bodies lined the border and by the color of their military uniforms, Asher knew they were Adani soldiers. Drones floated over the rugged terrain and they saw Adani soldiers on their feet, moving fast, retreating.

Asher stole a look at King Luang who watched on with narrowed eyes. "We caught them by surprise, but make no mistake—tomorrow will be different. The king will know we've banded together now. He'll know Santina is not alone, and he'll need to make a big statement to make it clear he will not be threatened," he said with pained eyes.

He returned his attention to the screen.

"His next move will not be subtle, Asher," the Queen of Arinia agreed.

"Then we'll retaliate, and continue to do so until he is defeated," Asher said. "I won't live in fear of Adani and I will not let them take my kingdom. They have started this, but we will finish it."

King Luang gave a small smile and his eyes looked a little less pained. "You're so much like him. You have his fighting spirit." His eyes darkened. "And you're going to need it. We all will."

Asher shook his hand. "Thank you for standing beside me."

"Killing Martin was Adani's biggest mistake. They murdered my friend, and I can't stand by and let them get away with that. We fight together."

Asher turned to the Queen of Arinia, who nodded.

King Luang looked to his security, who prepared to escort them to the waiting helicopters. They'd agreed to stay together for the initial attack, but now Asher had to return home to Santina. He needed to be there for his people.

ASHER

"What would you do now if you were the Adani king?" Asher asked as he buckled himself in.

James chewed on his cheek then sighed heavily. "I would teach you a lesson and hit you where it hurts most."

"My family?" Asher asked.

"Your extended family," James clarified. "King Khalil will hit the city—or at least that's what I'd do. Not all of the Adani soldiers were killed at the border, and some of them would've made their way into Santina. He might use them to coordinate an attack, but I don't think it'll be big enough."

"He can't poison the water supply. We put your additional measures in place," Asher said.

"I don't think he'll be that subtle. You need to watch your airspace—that's how I'd retaliate."

As if on cue, the helicopter bounced and Asher clutched the hand rests before exhaling a shaky breath.

James continued, unfazed. "And while you're focused on that, he'll move in his soldiers from every side."

Asher met his gaze. "I need to give him a distraction of his own."

A plan was formulating in Asher's mind. If he hadn't already started the war, what he was thinking would have done so in spectacular fashion.

He leaned back and prayed for a smooth flight. He prayed for a few minutes of sleep too, but all he could see when he closed his eyes was the image of fallen men. It didn't matter that they were Adani soldiers—they were still men following orders of a corrupt and violent king. They shouldn't have to die for a man who wouldn't die for them. But that was beyond Asher's control. If he hadn't fought back, he would be seeing dead Santinians when he closed his eyes.

One of his prayers was answered and the turbulence faded, replaced by a rhythmic hum. Asher drifted off to sleep, knowing he would need it, because it might be the last sleep he'd have for a while.

* * *

IN THE BLINK OF AN EYE, they'd landed on the Bennetts' helicopter pad and Asher was shaken awake before being ushered inside.

"Everything is ready for the press conference," James said.

"Good," Asher said, heading in the direction of the room he'd requested be set up: a live speech to be broadcast over Santina's television network. The palace was in shambles and the balcony had been blown up, so that wasn't an option, and they didn't want to invite media into the Bennetts' home. A broadcast was the safest option.

Asher's eyebrows lifted when he walked into the room. A painting of the Santinian flag had been hung on the wall. It was the exact painting that hung behind Asher's desk—his father's desk.

William entered, his eyes following Asher's. He sighed. "They're a matching pair, those paintings. I had them made for your father's birthday one year. And then after everything that happened . . . I couldn't bring myself to get rid of it, but I also couldn't look at it every day. It has been wrapped up and stored in our basement until tonight."

"Thank you," Asher said, placing one hand on William's shoulder. "I'm glad you kept it."

William smiled. "Me too. I certainly did not foresee needing it for such an occasion."

Asher nodded as he moved to stand behind the desk. He took a calming breath as a crew member counted down to zero.

"Santina," Asher said, looking directly into the camera, "the day has come to defeat our enemy—the one who has been hiding in the shadows. *Adani.*"

Asher narrowed his eyes, taking a moment to let that name sink in.

"Adani was once our friend, but they are greedy, and they want what they cannot have: Santina. I told you I would not be blackmailed and that I would destroy anyone who threatened Santina. So, I am telling you this: King Khalil is your enemy. He planned to do to Santina what he did to his poor many years ago—poison their water system and kill them off."

Asher could almost hear the gasps of his people.

"I don't make these accusations lightly, and I don't make them without evidence. King Khalil is corrupt, violent, and he will stop at nothing to get what he wants. We will not tolerate this any longer! And we do not stand alone—Santina has friends who will back us and fight with us on every border. My father fought so hard to avoid a war, and this was not a decision I made lightly. But while my father didn't see the heinous acts Adani is capable of, you will—I will expose the Adani to the world. There will be no mercy!"

He took a long breath.

"A war has started, and we will fight alongside our allies to defeat our common enemy. We may be small, Santina, but underestimating us was Adani's biggest mistake. We will fight, we will advance, and we will be victorious!" Asher locked his eyes on the camera, not afraid to reveal the emotion in his eyes. He meant every word and he would fight for Santina until his last breath.

When the cameras stopped rolling, Asher realized Abi was there, standing against the wall, her face unreadable.

He moved toward her, ignoring everyone else, before stopping a step in front of her.

"Strong, brave, and honest, King Asher," she said with a smile.

He returned the smile tightly. "But what do you think, Abi?"

Her eyebrows threaded together. "I just told you what I thought."

Asher nodded. "I know this is going to be hard," he said. "This war goes against everything you stand for."

She took his hands, threading her fingers through his. "I stand for righting the wrongs in the world. Do I like war? No, I don't. But do I like Adani murdering innocent people? No, I don't," she said flatly, looking into his eyes. "I told you I would stand beside you and support you. That doesn't change now. If you go to war, I'll grab my gun and stand beside you. Forever." She turned her hand so her engagement ring shone.

"Thank you," Asher told her quietly, and he truly meant it. Her support had never meant more to him than it did in that moment. "Let's get out of here," he said, looking over his shoulder for security.

They surrounded them in seconds and escorted them to a bedroom.

Asher found a new toothbrush in the bathroom, cleaned his teeth, and threw his suit on the floor. He crawled into bed, settled his head on the pillow, and pulled Abi into his arms. He exhaled, sighing with relief. It had been a hellish twenty-four hours, but they were safe, and he could finally close his eyes for the night.

* * *

His cell phone ringing on the bedside table startled him from his sleep. When he saw the name on the screen, he knew it wasn't going to be good news.

"James," Asher said quickly.

"Adani has retaliated," James said, his words rushing into each other. "They hit the holy site, the Lithe Ruins."

Asher's blood froze in his veins as he tried to process what James was telling him.

"How did they do that without being detected by our radar?" Asher asked, his voice strained.

"They *were* detected," James said tersely. "Your military tried to shoot them down, but it was too late. They'd already launched the missile."

Asher pulled at his shirt like it was strangling him. He sat upright, swinging his legs out of bed. "How bad is it?"

"It's a catastrophic, fiery blaze, Asher. There will be nothing left of the Ruins."

Asher leaned forward, shaking with fury as he rested his elbows on his knees and hung his head.

He drew a long breath, and then another. "I'll call you back." He ended the call and paced the length of the bedroom. He knew where to hit Adani hardest, but he wouldn't make that decision without King Luang's consent.

He dialed his number. "I assume you're not calling with good news," King Luang answered.

"Adani has hit the Lithe Ruins—the holy site I refused to sell them. If I wasn't going to give it to them, they were going to make sure I couldn't have it, either."

There was a long pause. Then, "What do you want to do now?"

"We will attack the royal compound. Reed is in place," Asher said, his voice shaking with rage. "It is time for Adani to fall."

THE STORY CONTINUES...

The fourth book of The Royals will be released late 2020.

In the meantime, you can begin James Thomas's story in *ESCANTA*, Book One of the James Thomas Series.

ALSO BY BROOKE SIVENDRA

THE JAMES THOMAS SERIES
    Escanta
    Saratani
    Sarquis
    Lucian
    Sorin
    The Favour

THE DEACON THOMAS DUET
    The Ranger
    The Redemption

THE THOMAS SECURITY SERIES
    The Vault
    The Traitor
    The Conspirator

THE SOUL SERIES
    The Secrets of Their Souls
    The Ghosts of Their Pasts
    The Blood of Their Sins

DID YOU ENJOY THIS BOOK? YOU CAN MAKE A BIG DIFFERENCE

Reviews are the most powerful tools in my arsenal when it comes to getting attention for my books. As much as I'd like to, I don't have the financial support of a New York publisher. I can't take out full page ads in the newspaper or put posters on the subway (not yet, anyway).

But I do have something much more powerful and effective than that, and it's something those publishers would kill to get their hands on.

A committed and loyal group of readers.

Honest reviews of my books help bring them to the attention of other readers.

If you've enjoyed this book I would be so grateful if you could spent just a few minutes leaving a review (it can be as short as you like). You can jump right to the page by clicking here.

Thank you so much.

ABOUT THE AUTHOR

Brooke Sivendra lives in Adelaide, Australia with her husband and two furry children. She has a degree in Nuclear Medicine and worked in the field of medical research before writing her first novel.

You can connect with Brooke at any of the channels listed below and she personally responds to every comment and email.
www.brookesivendra.com
brooke@brookesivendra.com
Facebook: www.facebook.com/bsivendra
Twitter: www.twitter.com/brookesivendra
Instagram: www.instagram.com/brookesivendra
Pinterest: www.pinterest.com/brookesivendra

Lightning Source UK Ltd.
Milton Keynes UK
UKHW011833181221
395882UK00001B/249